DJERI

DJERI

And Other Stories

Sandra M Mallia

PARTRIDGE
A Penguin Random House Company

ISBN:	Hardcover	978-1-4828-3067-5
	Softcover	978-1-4828-3068-2
	eBook	978-1-4828-3069-9

Print information available on the last page.

To order additional copies of this book, contact
Toll Free 800 101 2657 (Singapore)
Toll Free 1 800 81 7340 (Malaysia)
orders.singapore@partridgepublishing.com

www.partridgepublishing.com/singapore

Contents

For my parents, who let me find my own way.

Preface

This is my town. These are my people. The framework for this place and its inhabitants has come from my imagination. The bricks and mortar have been gathered from snippets of information found across Australia. This is not real, yet it is all real, for readers might catch a momentary glimpse of themselves or their neighbours in this town where secrets are revealed. The hidden lives and the problems in this community could belong anywhere or to anyone.

When I first learned that we had around eight hundred Indigenous Australians living in and around our small community, I wondered where and who they were, what they did, and what they looked like. Digging deeper out of curiosity, I discovered that they existed amongst my own circle of friends and relatives and that some had chosen to keep their histories private. They remained invisible by choice.

Those histories must remain private, but I have used this knowledge that they do exist to construct other stories encompassing the problems encountered by people who have lived with fear and intolerance, whether real or imagined, at some stage in their lives.

Fictional observers, who can only relate to what they see or hear, tell most of these stories. They cannot know the deep, personal feelings of those Indigenous folk who, for various reasons, prefer to remain anonymous, often hiding behind their European names and pale skin. I want the reader to understand that these characters are not secretive because they are ashamed of their heritage but because it is easier to live without the need to explain, without the labels that are automatically attached to persons of colour.

Some of the characters did not learn of their ancestral backgrounds until late in life. A generation ago, there were things people did not talk about, were not willing to admit, even to their own children. To suddenly learn that your relatives are not blood related can be disturbing, but for Amelia's family, it meant the loss of a lifetime of opportunities. For the poet it was too late, his relatives lost long ago with their stories and their sense of belonging, in the Tasmanian social wilderness. His only hope was that the archival digging he started would continue to unearth histories that could give him a meaningful place to eventually lay his bones.

For Tayo, his quest to be accepted eventually came undone. His blood relatives cared enough to visit, but whether the townsfolk could forgive his lies was uncertain. Kyle loved his life and searched incessantly for anything that connected him to his Indigenous heritage, although there had been dark times when secrets were kept and the truth was avoided. Gabby knew the importance of her father's words, and it was his story that came closest to the truth about lives hidden beneath manufactured histories of Indigenous families.

I have gathered all of my constructed, small-town citizens and given them a place in semi-rural Victoria. They inhabit the schools, the shopping malls, the cafes, and the buses of this rapidly progressing, imagined town that I have built on Melbourne's outskirts.

Bear

Bear is a big fella. Quiet-like. Doesn't say much, but when he speaks, softly, like he doesn't care to be noticed, you can hear the private-school accent tainted a little by years in the trucking business.

He was just a little tacker when his parents took him in, brother to the others who didn't have his skin colour. Knew about his birth mother but for a long time had no need to find her. Wasn't until the kids arrived that he went looking. Now he drives trucks between here and Sydney, where his other family live. He knows he's not allowed, but sometimes he has to take the children. They understand that whenever the flashing lights come screaming up behind them, they must hide, tuck themselves away in the cramped sleeping compartment. You would not think such little kids could know so much. Not a peep out of them, and he's a conscientious driver when the kids are there, has no fear of breathalysers. Other truckies keep him informed, sometimes closing the convoy tight, protective, reinforcing the brotherhood. A truck alone is vulnerable, but all together they are daunting, powerful.

Bear took on his kids alone. They are not even his kids really. He moved in with his girlfriend, and she moved out. He kind of inherited them, just babies at the time, two of them, one blacker than him, the other white. The little one, the white one, he calls Whitey Wag Tail because she is always hopping around like that little bird, scolding him for his slackness, chattering, friendly. Had to keep his eye on that one.

Soon they will be starting school, and he worries a little about filling out forms, facing authority. How do you explain parentage? Make it all up?

Nobody knows. Nobody can tell. Have to move out of this town, take them to Sydney, and kind of mix them up with their cousins. Whitey will be a problem though, and he'll miss his other parents, siblings, and the town where he feels comfortable.

Of course, there are the local hecklers—always have been, always will be. He learned there's an advantage sometimes in showing your ancestry. People say, "He's black, what do you expect?" and they leave him alone. Bear can take that. He knows which side is his and doesn't care what others see. Never mind his expensive education, gentile upbringing, or that passive tolerance passed down through the generations. Bear just is.

He still visits his adoptive mum and dad. Sometimes, she takes the kids, but her age is telling and things are really difficult, especially as Whitey is so active. The kids are his boori now, his little people and his responsibility, according to the rules of his new northern family. He has no regrets. "Things are as they are," he would say, and Whitey scolds because he won't stand up for himself.

Sometimes, he is questioned by outsiders. It is difficult trying to avoid confrontation in a small town where everybody knows everybody else's business, and local people won't rock the boat, won't tell the questioners more than they need to know. That's how he gets to keep the kids, cocooned amongst people who fear being labelled discriminatory, racist, protected by their silence.

The day will come when someone will report him, and then they will be taken from him. He feels safer in Sydney, where they seem anonymous amongst their own. Whitey is a problem though.

Djeri

Jeri is ten years old. His mum is a single parent, and he doesn't really know who his dad is. He walks home from school alone, kicking at pebbles or walking with his head in the air while watching birds in the nature strip trees, his fair hair hanging long across his shoulders.

That's how we met. He bumped into me, startling us both, his deep, brown eyes wide with uncertainty. He knows my face from the school, where I am an occasional teacher. Now we talk some afternoons, just a brief chat where he tells me how he went at school. Asks me questions I cannot answer.

His father was gone before he was born. There had been others when he was little because his mum said he needed a dad. It was sometimes OK, before her darker relatives came visiting, pushing the boundaries of friendship, making the truth visible. Jeri remembers the taunts from his new dads, the smell of alcohol, the hospital visits, and the department always checking on them.

Cut off his hair and he's nothing but a bloody abo. Can't change him.

That's when they moved back down from Sydney and Mum started telling him that the stories were secret, just for the two of them.

It's better that way.

Doesn't really know much about his ancestors, just picked up bits and pieces from his mother. How not so long ago they came from the cold southern lands, dressed in possum-skin cloaks, speaking a language lost when the clans from Scotland cleared the Gippsland bush. He didn't really believe it anyway; after all, he was fair like his mum. She told him that's where he got his name. DJeri, little bird, Jeri for the records.

Sometimes, when he's sick, she brings in the gum leaves for him to smell, finds some milky-white sap to heal his itches, or makes a tea from some plant that fixes his stomachache. She just knows all that stuff. He tells his friends, and they say she is a witch. She's OK with that.

Better a witch than a darkie.

She says she doesn't want the handouts, doesn't want to be labelled. She thinks that a single mum like her is vulnerable, and if anything goes wrong, they will take him away.

Just keep it quiet, Jeri. It's just for us to know.

He says she is always worrying. She remembers the stories from her grandmother about the children being taken. Didn't know her own mum. Said she couldn't handle the arguments with the department and just gave up. Left her in foster homes until her grandmother found her and took her north. She says that now Gramma has gone, she and Jeri must look after each other. She knows times have changed, yet still the fear remains.

He listened to the stories, but they were separate from him. He was just like his friends: white, belonging to this town and not to the earth like she told him. She told him about the Kurnai and the Kulin, the Wurundjeri and the earthen rings worn into the hillside just west of the town. She told him dreamtime stories at night to put him to sleep, stories she had heard from her grandmother. She told him it was natural for their people to tell stories and that was how they kept their clans together, learning the unwritten rules.

But he must keep his silence. Why was his mother afraid?

After a time, he saw no harm in elaborating on them at school, inventing relatives who could be heroes, inventing places that had some eerie significance. They were just stories, and it was OK to tell stories.

Did she really expect him to keep quiet? His stories, his growing knowledge of indigenous words and history, made him popular, important. Sometimes, the children would chant those newly learned words, the rhythm and mystery rolling off their tongues. Yet he remained alone, a loner.

There'd been an incident in the schoolyard, a fight, and Jeri was the instigator as far as they could tell, living inside his stories.

Acting out the Warrigal, the wild blacks defending their land.

After that, Teacher said he was not allowed to tell stories that were not true. He had to respect the ways of Indigenous Australians and understand that those stories belonged to them. He should not take them as his own. Jeri told his mum, and her fear showed through the anger.

But they are of the Koori, our people.

This time they would stay. They had finished with moving, and she knew that Jeri must be allowed to find his own way. Was she protecting herself or the boy? Better to be angry than afraid.

Now he draws the stories in the dusty playground and then explains them quietly to anyone who will listen. He tells them as though they belong to him. The more he talks about them, the more he feels they are his. He tells them in secret to his friends, and they are in awe with the mystery, with doing something illegal, and afraid of the spirits that will reprimand them if they let it slip that they've been listening.

He was beginning to understand that he had a right to claim these stories out loud, and this confused him. He came to recognize others like him at school, the dark pools of eyes giving them away. "We are Italian, Greek, or even Polynesian," they would say. "That's where our skin colour comes from."

We are not Indigenous.

I found him one morning on my early sunrise walk. Saw him standing on the brink of an ancient ring, worn into the hillside by years of ceremonial gatherings, eons of stories in song and movement. It is significant now only as a wasted block where a house could be built, rendered and painted in pastel colours just like the neighbours. Where a garden could be laid with river pebbles imported from Asia, planted with the newly popular structural trees and shrubs. It is fenced in, unavailable.

I could smell the eucalypts, their scarlet flowers scattered across the dry earth after a night's feasting from flying foxes. A small mob of kangaroos bounded silently away as the town slowly stirred with the rising day. Somehow, it seemed right for him to be here alone, and I did not wish to interfere.

For a brief moment, I saw his hand poised in front of his face, the other hand bent behind as he danced a few steps, hindered by the unkempt kangaroo grass and his own sense of secrecy. Jeri stopped when he saw me and quietly slipped between the grassy furrows, out of sight. I knew then where his heritage lay and knew that I would listen more genuinely to his stories from that day. His mother was right. He is of the earth, and nothing can change that.

Tayo

You must understand. This is a small town, and it took guts to start a business back then. Yeah, sure, he had his future father-in-law's backing, but at first, there was little to do at the yard. He'd close up early and spend his afternoons at the Arms with me and the rest of his mates.

After he married Sal, things picked up a little. She's a good worker. Straightened him out for a while, and the town grew, so he sold more cars. But the drink had done its damage long before the kids came along. Despite that, he's a good businessman with an eye for a bargain, and he never cheated his mates. Sal managed his money. Picked him up at all hours from the pub and raised those kids without his help.

He's always been called Tayo. Think his real name was Theodore or something. Anyway, he married into money, but in this town, he still had to earn respect. Back then, everybody knew everybody else, so when he started to go downhill, there was always a helping hand to pull him back out of the shit.

That's the point, you see. He never forgot and would pay back those who stood by him, so he's respected to this day, and Sal has stayed with him through it all. Then the oldest boy started to get into trouble. Caught him once shooting up in the ladies toilets at St Albans Railway Station. They've tried all the wonder cures, transfusions, psychiatrists, spiritual stuff, but he'll never change, and now Sal looks after his kids. Made Tayo look to his own problems, and he knew he'd done them wrong. Swore he'd do better for the grandchildren.

Trouble is he just tried too hard to fit in, wanted to mix it with the boys, be part of the crowd, so to speak. Might have been better if he'd just stayed himself. You know it wasn't until he had the accident and ended up in hospital that we found out where he'd come from. I suppose it was partly our fault because we just knew him as Sal's man and never really asked about his other family. It seemed unimportant somehow, and he never volunteered any information. Sal and the kids, the car yard, his mates, and the booze were his whole life. And we … Well, we never questioned that. As I said, this is a small town and a person's privacy is respected.

So there we were, bringing him flowers and stuff into the hospital, him with his leg all bandaged and that morphine drip stuck in his arm. He was pretty messed up and having a bad time without the drink, you see, so I don't think he even knew we were there when this other bloke walked in. Said he was Tayo's cousin come down from Echuca after the nurse had contacted him.

We just stood there with our mouths open for a bit while he politely held out his hand, until one of the guys started laughing. Not just a bit of a laugh but a big, belly-rolling laugh, and then he said to this bloke that he was in the wrong ward. He said Tayo couldn't be his cousin, that they didn't even look alike. The nurse came in then and asked us all to leave because we were too loud, but he stayed, and when I looked back, he was just standing there looking kind of sadly down at Tayo.

Try to understand that it came as a bit of a shock to us when this big, black bloke in his fancy moleskins and R. M. Williams boots just walks in and announces that he is Tayo's cousin. How could we have known? We were never told, and I guess we had no reason to ask.

The Poet

He's an old man now, lost in his dreams. He sits on the southern slope amongst the lichen-encrusted rocks on a cold winter's day, notebook in hand, scribbling sad words with a chewed pencil. The early days come back to him, carried by a brutal wind that tears through the ripped parka and slithers into chilled ears tucked beneath a work-weary beanie.

Tasmania's west coast, constantly hammered by driving rains that beat holes into the coastal sands and tore at the toughened vegetation on the rocky slopes, spawned those memories of a secretive and bitter childhood. Here, on the mainland, he fights with the wind spirits who would take his mind before the stories of his people are found.

****

Thomas Riley saved his pennies and left the island at the first opportunity, celebrating his sixteenth birthday on a rickety fishing vessel en route to the mainland. He settled on these barren acres outside Melbourne even before he had become a man, exchanging money only after he had reached the legal age. Now, more than half a century later, through the broken fences and empty paddocks, he sees the green forests and deep, wooded chasms vaguely swirling from the grey mists of childhood.

He remembers his parents, taken by the wild sea that had provided a living. His old mind struggles to recall what they had told him about his grandparents, the sealers who settled with the Aboriginal women and the communities who refused to be rounded up and moved to the island reserves.

He remembers the teacher who took him in and traded him to a farmer for a few sheep, his first angry secret. It seemed to him that the sun never warmed that mountain farm, and no friendly voices comforted him. To ease the cold silence, Thomas sometimes sang to the rhythm of the axe as he prepared the evening's firewood or hummed as he milked the old house-cow, his head resting on her warm flank. When no one could hear, he sang the songs taught by his mother, using the words of his ancestors, forbidden by the churches and the schools that he sometimes attended.

It was at school that he learned his people no longer existed, that Truganini was the last of the natives, and the records showed no others. He understood his grandfathers had been fishermen from the old country, setting up their industry on the windswept south-western shores, but they were aided by the women of Trowerner and left dark-skinned children with Irish names.

Those children and most of their children after them had never left the island, yet they were not counted as native, remaining hidden with their histories. He has spent these last years searching archives, questioning authorities, revisiting the Tasmanian farms and families who held his secrets. Proving his existence, wiping out his shame.

****

The old man pulls his jacket tighter against the gusting wind and scribbles his rage quickly, before the words are forgotten.

I was there.
Didn't you see me?
I am the little roo
come down from Tarner,
the creation spirit.
I am the Palawa.
My stories are hidden
Where the sun

Lifts the winds over the mountains.

Thomas Riley had soaked up the strength given to him by the stories he uncovered, and still he kept searching. He had found his heritage, only to have it torn apart by those who thought they could choose who was Aboriginal and who wasn't. "You are Palawa," they told him. "You are a true Aboriginal elder and cannot be anything else." "My name says otherwise," he told them, "and there are others like me who will not be ignored."

We are the Lia Pootah
Come down from the women of Trowerner.
Ours is a kinship
born of many nations.
We will not be hidden
by Palawa dreaming.

Thomas Riley makes a decision and tears out the last pages before placing his notebook under a time-pitted rock. He carefully runs a finger over the written words, smoothing away a lifetime of secrets. The stories will find their own way now that he has started the digging. He stands for a moment watching the pages tremble in the wind, his old hands restricting their freedom, before releasing them to the spirits that whistle across the basalt plains and shriek through the city streets.

I am Palawa.
We are the Lia Pootah.

Jedda's Mother

Jedda lives alone in a modest weatherboard on the boundary between the two shires. His house is run down, and the garden has been taken over by discarded furniture, white goods, and fallen branches. Jedda's mother, a semi-retired teacher, lives up the road a bit in a neat two-storey home set on an impersonal, landscaped acre. She brings him his dinner each night, and he complains that he doesn't like whatever it is, putting it in the fridge with all the other uneaten meals. She tries to keep him living, although at times, she feels the effort is just too great.

Jedda is unwell. His mother tells everyone it is prescription pills that he takes for his depression, but she has seen the bowls with green remnants stuck to their base, the blackened plastic bottles with pieces of hose attached. She recognizes that sweet, musty odour when he opens the door and notes the seedlings just sprouted on the kitchen windowsill. She does not tell him she knows, and he continues doing what he has always done.

Sometimes he gets angry. The neighbours turn a blind eye because they know they are in no danger. Jedda's phobia prevents him from leaving the house to do them any harm, and his anger is usually silent except for the purging of household goods. From behind their dusty venetians, they watch as he stands just inside the front door and throws another piece of his wasted life out into the long grass. His mother collects the unbroken crockery, casserole dishes, and cutlery on her way out each day, takes them home to wash, and stacks them in boxes until he gets better.

His mother blames his father for the weaknesses. Says she never should have married a blackfella. Three sons and none of them any good. One still lives at home, sits around all day watching TV while she does his cooking and washing. At least she knows where he is and what he is doing. Sometimes he visits his brother, but she does not encourage it because he always comes back with glazed eyes and a voracious appetite. Jedda could do with the boy's support, but she has trouble choosing between the two sons. At least the youngest of the three has a job, although she worries about those scrawny kids of his and the bruises on his girlfriend's shoulder. She could encourage the girl to leave, but then she will be left with him to look after, and Jedda is her priority at the moment.

When they were born, she gave them fancy English names—Gerard, Crighton, and Harris—to balance their Australian colour and protect them from the bullies at school. It wasn't long before their names were changed to Jedda, Critta, and Harry and it was the others who needed protection. Their father only made it worse when he fronted up to the principal, worse for wear after a long day at the pub. She heard the staff gossip and the comments of "Typical. What did you expect? They are all the same" or "No wonder the kids are like they are." She felt like reminding them that the boys had two parents but thought it was better to keep her mouth shut.

Their father had left when the boys were in secondary school, and none of them bothered to find him. It was easier, for a time, without him. When Jedda left school and started work, his mother was pleased and preferred to ignore the occasional slurring of speech, the money he borrowed from her despite earning his own. She packed his lunch each morning in neat Tupperware containers, kept his work trousers pressed, and his collars clean. Jedda complained when she polished his heavy boots. He scuffed them in the dust to make them acceptable.

When he started bringing those girls home, she bought the little weatherboard place and moved him in, with conditions that have never been kept. There is always a reason why he cannot pay the bills or keep the garden tidy, so she takes on tutoring after school hours to help him, hoping he will think about the extra work she does for him. Hoping it will make him look closer at his own problems. She can never understand why those girls refused to care for Jedda and the house the way she does. Just in case they had other intentions, she kept her inheritance private, telling the boys that the money from her parents' estate had been left to charity.

After the last girl left, taking the baby and stacking the car with the few valuable things he treasured, Jedda closed the door and went to bed. His mother found him days later, trembling under the grimy covers, a mouldy pizza beside the bed with half-smoked cigarettes stuffed into empty drink cans with strange names and potent ingredients.

For the next few months, she sits with him in the hours before and after work, talking but receiving only vague and angry answers. She is afraid each morning as she opens his door that she will find him lying overdosed on the floor and she will have to make a decision. She wonders how she will explain it to other people. If only she knew where the pills and the green stuff came from, she might be able to eliminate one problem. Her suggestions of doctors, counsellors, or moving back home only meet with abuse and ramblings about how she had turned his father out of the house and gave his younger brothers more attention. She knows it is only his condition making him talk that way and continues doing what she always does.

Sometimes she thinks he might be better off if she gives up the effort to keep him in his sad, violent world.

Jedda's mother walks the short distance home each evening. She talks out loud to herself, reflecting on the small improvements she sees in her eldest son. Today he showered and changed his clothes, throwing the dirty ones onto the front grass for her to carry home and wash. He ate some of the fruit she had left in a gingham-lined basket on the kitchen table. Tonight she might be able to do something for herself without worrying about Gerard.

She prepares the evening meal for Crighton and bakes a cake for his snacks tomorrow, hangs out the day's washing, wipes down the second bathroom, and sorts through the day's mail. She takes a bottle of port from behind the flour crock in the pantry, picks out her favourite wine glass, and heads off to bed, tired but certain she has made all the right decisions. As she passes the hallstand, she hesitates momentarily before picking up the little, gilt-framed, family photo taken when the boys were just babies, and she was happy with her husband.

She arranges these items carefully on the bedside table before showering and combing her hair. In clean, fresh pyjamas, she props the pillows higher and fills her glass. She finds a bottle of pills in the drawer and climbs into bed, kissing her fingers and transferring those kisses to the photo.

The little, brown faces smile up at her as she swallows the nightly capsule, easing it down with the velvety smooth port. Tonight she will sleep peacefully, believing that her eldest son will survive another day.

Jedda

"Answer the frickin' phone, you moron." Jedda held the toilet door open a fraction and yelled angrily at his younger brother.

Critta stayed put in his usual position, half-asleep in front of the television, surrounded by empty cans and pizza boxes that lay scattered over the coffee table and the floor beside the grubby couch.

"And turn off the telly. Who do you think pays the bloody bills around here anyway?"

"Not you, that's for sure," Critta mumbled sourly as the phone cut out and his brother slammed the toilet door shut.

Within minutes, the phone started to ring again, and Jedda cursed his way out of the toilet, yanking his jeans up over thin, scabby legs. Critta snickered, grabbing the phone before his brother reached the table.

"Tell you what, bro, you learn to wash your hands, and I'll feel a lot better letting this phone touch my ear. Here, you take it, and by the way, we all know who pays your bills. Without Mum, you'd be dead. You'd be holed up in this dump too shit-scared to leave, and you'd starve to death."

"Why don't you just shut up and get out of here? Go back to Mummy's house so she can spoon-feed you, frickin idiot."

Jedda struggled to zip up with one hand as he held the phone to his ear. He could hear a voice on the other end even before he answered. He moved the phone away from his face and stood looking doubtfully at it for several moments before replacing it on its cradle.

"What did you do that for? Why didn't you answer? Who was it?" Critta demanded.

Jedda just looked at him, saying nothing for a while, and then hesitantly answered his brother. "It was the old man, I think."

"You think? Our dad you mean? How do you know when you didn't even answer?"

"I heard enough. I remember his voice."

The phone rang again, vibrating out of its cradle and cracking open as it hit the floor.

Jedda grabbed it up to his ear, holding it together with both hands and speaking through his fingers. "Hello? Dad? Can you hear me?"

A slurred voice came through, and Jedda listened with squinting eyes, concentrating hard to understand before the phone cut out completely.

"I think he said he's coming round."

"Fuck, Jedda. We don't want him here. He hasn't bothered to call for fifteen years. What's the point now?" Critta glanced around the room. "And what the hell is he going to think of this place anyhow?"

Critta grabbed a black plastic garbage bag from a pile of junk in the corner, held it under the small table, and scraped in the rubbish. He picked up cans and food cartons, a couple of improvised bongs, plates that had been used as ash trays, some dirty T-shirts, and socks, filling the bag with anything he could find.

"Leave it!" Jedda yelled at him. "You don't care anyway, and if he is that keen to see us, then he can see us just as we are."

Critta took a greasy dishcloth from the kitchen and wiped the table, leaving food smears across the pockmarked veneer. "I still don't care about him. I just don't want him to think that we are like him. Bloody alky abo, that's all he is. Went walkabout just when Mum needed some help around the place."

"Jesus, Critta. Do you really think you're any better, sitting around all day watching telly, on the dole and not lifting a finger to help? Go and look in the mirror, bro, before you start picking on Dad."

"Why the hell are you defending him? Don't you remember when he used to turn up at school, stinking of alcohol and threatening the principal? Worse still were those days when he'd be waiting for us after school, hanging over the fence, sucking on a stubby, and trying to chat up all the girls. God, he's even more of a loser than you with your stupid phobias. And while we're at it, do you really think Mum doesn't know about your dope and that stash of pills? She's not stupid, you know."

Critta dragged the bag out to the wheelie bin, picking up bits and pieces of rubbish along the way. He looked at the junk distributed under the bushes and across the porch, shaking his head as though seeing it for the first time. Jedda watched him from the safety of the doorway.

"Could have helped me tidy things up a bit before this, you know. I've been crook, and all you do is come around and pinch me beer, you and your mates. Piss off and nick Harry's stuff for a change. Who needs you anyway?"

"We've been through all this shit before, Jedda. You know why Harry won't have me round there. He's ashamed I'll notice things, like how scared of him his kids are. He's ashamed that he's no different from you and me, and he thinks that Mum has no time for him, that she doesn't like him."

The argument between the two of them was over as they focused on their younger brother and the problems he tried to hide from them. Jedda pulled a stool into the open doorway and sat down with a smoke, offering the packet to his brother who at first declined.

"Nup. Giving up that stuff." He stalled for a while before accepting the offer and sitting down on the porch steps, mumbling something about going cold turkey.

Minutes later, Harry's Ute pulled into the driveway, narrowly missing the warped picket fence and clipping the overflowing bin, sending some of its contents back into the grass where they had originated. The two men stood in surprise and swore in unison as Harry jumped out of the car to check the damage. Another man emerged more slowly from the passenger seat, stepped over the rubbish, and headed up the narrow path, appraising the house and yard as he walked.

"Harris warned me about this place, but I didn't expect it to be this bad. Hello, boys. Remember me?" The older man stood waiting for a response, and when it didn't come, he moved uninvited into the house.

"Your mum contacted me a while back. Said she couldn't manage you lot anymore and that she thought it was about time I faced my responsibilities. Might be too late by the look of things here. Aren't you going to say hello to your old man?"

"You look different. That's all." Jedda spoke quietly, eyeing his dad's tidy appearance and polished boots.

"Went into rehab five years ago and never looked back, kiddo. I wrote to your mother back then and have kept in contact occasionally since, but she seemed to be doing OK without me, so I thought it was better for me to butt out and let her manage things. Guess I was wrong."

"Why didn't you write to us? Why didn't she tell us?" Critta's voice rose, the anger obvious in his reddened cheeks and furrowed brow.

"Now don't get mad at your mother. She thought she was doing the right thing, and I don't blame her for not trusting me after all I put her through."

"And now you expect us to trust you, I suppose." Critta turned to Jedda for support but was met with a bewildered stare.

"Crighton, I'm sorry for what I did in the past, but that's all over now. I wasn't sure whether or not I should come down from the Murray, but now that I'm here, I'm staying. You need me, and we'll get you all back on track."

"You think you can just wipe out all those bad years? You treated us like shit all the time we were kids, drank away Mum's hard-earned money, and then just left without a word. We're doing OK without you, so piss off." Critta's voice began to break, the obvious emotion making him even angrier.

Harry yelled from the driveway that he'd done what he had to do and was leaving. Critta grabbed his jacket and hurried out the front door, calling to Harry to wait. He clambered into the front seat and wound down the window, shouting a warning to his older brother.

"He's all yours, Jedda. I'm not coming back until he's gone, and don't believe all that frickin shit he tells you."

The old man stood on the porch and called out as the Ute backed down the driveway, turning towards the town centre and Harry's rented unit.

"I'm staying, Crighton. I owe you. You're not getting rid of me that easily."

He turned to his eldest son, closing the door and looking for a clean place to sit. "Guess it's just you and me now, Gerard. We've got a lot to talk about, and it looks like I'm going to be here for a long time. Got a job on the roads, so money's no problem, and I pick up an old car on Monday. I'll deal with the other two later. Right now, you are my priority."

Jedda checked the room, hiding his cigarette papers, filters, and the bag of dried leaves He took the potted seedlings out and sheltered them behind the garage, his hands shaking with the sudden rush of effort. Back in the lounge, his father was quiet, watching the last footy quarter through the dust and handprints on the television screen. Deep in thought and with the early signs of panic showing in his eyes, Jedda decided to remove the slab of beer stashed in a corner, heaving it on his bony shoulders and tottering back out to the garage.

When he came back, his father was standing with a bottle of spirits in his hand. "You might as well hide this too, Gerard, if it's going to worry you that much. You'll soon see. I'm off the drink for good now. It wasn't easy at first, but believe me, I'm clean now. And I'll show you how it's done if you'll let me help. Now, where can I sleep tonight?"

"Ah geez, there's a spare bed in the back room, but it's all covered in junk, and there's no blankets. Are you sure you want to stay here? There's no food, nothing."

As father and son considered the options, the front door opened. Critta and Harry walked in without speaking and chucked some clean sheets, pillows, and doonas on the couch. Harry went back to the car and returned with a container of food. There were bread and milk, coffee and sugar, fruit salad, and a steaming casserole with boiled rice.

"Mum was waiting for you to call. She already had all this stuff packed and the dinner cooking, but just because we've brought it over doesn't mean we're fuckin happy about you coming back. What do you reckon, Critta?" For the first time that day, Harry sided with his brothers, looking rather pleased with himself for having made a point.

Critta walked over to his old man, his teeth clenched as he spoke. "People say we're like you, and they are probably bloody right. But it didn't have to be this way. You didn't have to embarrass us at school with your drinking and always thinking they had it in for you because you are black. Couldn't you see that it wasn't your dark skin that turned people against you? It was your behaviour. If you hadn't acted out the bad guy, they never would have blamed everything on your colour."

Critta trembled angrily as his father put his face close to that of his son and looked him directly in the eye.

"If that's the case, Crighton, how come you have no friends? I mean *real* friends. How come you have no job, and how come you act just like I did at your age? How come you didn't learn from your mother instead of copying what I did? You say colour has nothing to do with the way you were treated, but I know you don't really believe that."

Harry urged Critta to leave, but their father hadn't finished yet. "Listen to me. I learned the hard way that colour does matter. But it's how you manage your temper that earns respect. I was the one who was intolerant. I was the one with the chip on my shoulder, and I was the one who lost it every time someone looked my way. You are exactly the same. Just forget about what others think and get on with your life, all of you. You can't hide behind your colour forever, you know."

The brothers looked at one another, remaining silent for a time while their father picked up the bed linen and headed for the spare room.

Finally, Jedda stepped forward and broke the uneasy silence. "Here, Dad. Let me help. We'll get rid of the rubbish tomorrow, and you can stay as long as you like. Or at least until we can't frickin stand each other anymore. Right, guys?"

Critta didn't answer. Instead, he settled in his usual position on the couch, and for the first time in many months, Harry joined him, lifting the lid on the still warm casserole and inhaling deeply. *Tomorrow the work will begin. Always tomorrow.*

Amelia

"Sonia, look at this." Jackie sat cross-legged on the worn carpet, sorting through the musty photographs and letters she had found hidden at the back of the linen closet. "There's a letter from Aunt Flo to Mum. She must have written it before she died. You've gotta read this." A curious grin spread across her face as she handed the paper to her sister and continued rummaging through her mother's sepia-tinted memories with the help of her teenage children.

Sonia remained quiet for several minutes, reading the letter over and again. "Burn it," she said suddenly, crushing the paper and tossing it away from her younger sister. "There's probably no truth in it anyway. Auntie Flo always resented the way Mum enjoyed her life. She just wanted to put a damper on things."

Despite Sonia's protests, Jackie smoothed the crumpled letter and began to read it aloud to her two daughters.

> Dear Amelia,
> Since I moved back to New South Wales, we have had little time for each other, but now my affliction has made me reflect on all those things you should have been told years ago. There are matters that were not discussed in our parents' day, and although I am several years older than you, there are many details about which even I have no knowledge.

Jackie's children laughed and shoved each other affectionately, mimicking their great aunt's formality and feigning excitement over family secrets about to be unearthed. Aunt Sonia protested and demanded her sister put the letter down.

"Why Sonia!" Jackie exclaimed, her dark eyes shining with amusement at her sister's discomfort. "I do believe you are embarrassed by our wayward relatives."

"Just leave it alone, Jackie. What's past is past and bringing it all up now is ridiculous. Mum hid the letter for a reason. Think about your kids." At that remark, Sonia's wide-eyed nieces turned their attention to their irate aunt before begging Jackie to finish the letter.

> As you are aware, Amelia, I was born on the ship en route to Australia from Malta in 1912, and our parents had no more children for several years. Father came here with little experience or knowledge of farming but managed to find work on a sheep station in New South Wales. His decision was most unusual and brave, or perhaps foolhardy, for a Maltese migrant during those early years.
>
> From there, he moved on to other properties, taking Mother and I along. We lived on the stations wherever there were huts available, and Father learned his job from the Aboriginal stockmen he met along the way. At that time he held the darkies in high esteem and greatly admired their skills as horsemen and horsewomen, knowing he would never be their equal on the land.
>
> During the hard times he would go droving and was often away for several months. You must remember that Mother had come from Malta where families and friends supported each other on a daily basis, and the church played a big part in their lives. Out here, she was lonely. Neighbours were often hours away. A travelling minister would occasionally stop by, or a ragged swaggie looking for work would send her scurrying back into the house where she would hide in a corner, terrified and at the same time guilty that she must turn him away.

> Her isolation meant that she learned the language slowly, and we both spoke a kind of broken English influenced by the travelling black families who taught us how to survive in the savage outback.

Jackie stopped reading briefly as she had caught sight of her two daughters examining the whiteness of their upturned palms and their midwinter tans. They seemed aware of what was coming in their great aunt's letter. Jackie hesitated, glancing uncertainly back at her sister who was angrily immersed in filling plastic boxes with all the paraphernalia gathered during the old woman's recent, secretive years. *She has her grandfather's temper,* Jackie thought, *and no sense of humour. How different we are …*

> I remember one young Aboriginal man, tall and straight and handsome in his own way, would often visit Mother, bringing his siblings to play with me in the sheds and paddocks where we lived somewhere in the Murrumbidgee region. When Father returned, the young man disappeared, and we did not see him again for a long while. I missed the company of the children, but then you were born and our days did not seem so lonely anymore. You looked like me, Mother said, although the sun darkened your skin more rapidly, and your eyes were so black. We both inherited the curly hair and stocky build of our Maltese ancestors.

She turned the page, reading more slowly now as each word brought her closer to a discovery she was beginning to understand but wasn't sure she was ready to accept. Her voice softened, and the smile disappeared as she became more immersed in the words.

> Do you remember that this would prove difficult in later years as we had to live with the "foreigner" torment in Melbourne

> where Father found carpentry work? He sent us to a Catholic school where other Mediterranean children who looked like us would leave us alone. That was not to be as we were treated as "country bumpkins," and eventually we settled outside the city where farmers and townspeople could live in harmony. But I have gotten ahead of myself, as there are other reasons why we left the outback stations and moved south.

Jackie's teenagers were becoming restless and craved takeaway. They were so different from Sonia's sour-faced boys who had moved from their family home as teenagers and rarely visited their mother. They had suffered the teasing at school and now denied their own "greasy wog" heritage, their western suburban upbringing, and even their Catholic boys college education. Sonia seemed OK with this distancing, or "independence," as she called it, and frowned on Jackie's relaxed parenting methods. She never realised just how much like Aunt Florence she had become.

The writing had become a little erratic, perhaps as Flo's arthritic hands tired. Some words were illegible, so Jackie replaced them with her own constructions, but it did not matter as she thought she knew where the letter was heading.

> Dearest Amelia, you were always Mother's favourite, but you often managed to rub Father's feelings the wrong way. He had to take the sheep on the road again when winter rains failed, and the summer grass became tinder dry. My friends returned, as did their handsome brother, and they stayed for what seemed a long time. You were still a baby, I was only eight years old, and the weeks felt like years. Again, I was sorry to see them go, although I was pleased to have Father back to tell me stories about his home country and his adventures in, what he called, "this new heathen land."
>
> Amelia, please do not be shocked, and as I said previously, I do not know all the details. Mother was delivered of a son when

you were barely two years old. Our parents hardly spoke after that, and the child was with us for a very short time. In those days, people never discussed their concerns with the children, so I was kept in the dark and left to my own imagination. Our brother was taken by white people I did not recognize, and I never saw him again. I recall that he was much darker than you, and I began to comprehend the relationship between our mother and the man I believe was your real father.

You must understand that our father was just trying to protect us, and that is why he decided that we needed to move south into Victoria. Many men had relationships with the black women in our outback locality, but for a white, married woman to take up with an Aboriginal man was a sin that could not be forgiven, and so the evidence was removed. You were brown but not so dark that people would talk. Our brother had inherited his father's dusky skin colour and facial features, making the dalliance visible and therefore unacceptable. In Victoria, no one would know the truth, and we would be able to mix with other migrant families. After the war, when more Maltese migrants were granted assisted passage to Australia, Mother found friends who spoke her language, and the child was perhaps forgotten.

Jackie raised herself stiffly from between the boxes and piles of yellowed papers. She moved closer to the window and searched the darkening street where she had spent her childhood. A freshening breeze lifted the brittle curtains and delivered the familiar dry scent of eucalypts. Jackie shuddered as an unexpected feeling of alienation washed over her briefly. Once, as a child, a new neighbour had called her Jacky-Jacky and told her angrily that she should go back to the desert where she belonged. Not quite understanding, Jackie had told her Mother, who simply brushed it aside, without bothering to explain.

"We had an uncle, Sonia." Jackie turned back into the stuffy room and faced her sister, a slow smile washing away any lingering uncertainties. "We might even have cousins, and as he was younger than Mum or Aunt Flo, there's a possibility that he is still out there somewhere. Keep looking, kids, and we might find more stuff about him." The girls groaned and voiced their hunger, but Jackie did not want to leave the boxes of history with her older sister for fear that they might disappear, this time forever.

"We'll go, Mum. Just down the road, there's that bakery. We'll get something there." The girls unfurled their long, brown legs, shoved the boxes aside, and headed for the door. Jackie's eldest daughter turned cheekily to Sonia. "Might even ask that old guy about Grandma. He's been there forever and will know something for sure." She laughingly closed the door before her aunt could protest.

"It's not our uncle that concerns me, Jackie." Sonia sounded really worried now as she tried to explain her feelings about a past that Jackie seemed to find captivating and even exciting.

"It's Mum. You just don't understand that her illicit affairs could divide our family and lose us some friends."

"Affairs? God, Sonia, she only had one affair, and that was long after Dad died, wasn't it? Jacob had been a friend since we were little, so you can understand her turning to him for comfort." "And whatever else she desired," Jackie *almost* said, but she did not want to upset her sister any more than necessary.

Sonia sighed resignedly. "Read the rest of the letter, Jackie, before the kids come back."

Jackie turned to the last fragile page as Flo's reminiscences continued, although the handwriting was becoming even more shaky and difficult to read.

> You always were attracted to people with dark skin, and so it was no surprise to me that you befriended Jacob and spent many hours with him after school. I am sorry now, but at the time I was pleased when Father put a stop to your visits and eventually persuaded you to marry Thomas, fresh out from England. We all believed he was a decent young man who

would be good for you, and he really did try hard to make you happy.

I understand now why you could not settle down, were constantly restless. I truly thought that when your beautiful, fair-haired Sonia was born you would be content, but I recall it was not until Jacqueline came along that your smiles returned. It was so unfortunate that your dear, sad husband had retreated into himself and never really recovered his once happy life.

My dear Amelia, we all blamed you for his illness, but we came to understand that his mental state was simply an inability to adjust to our harsh landscape and an overwhelming desire to revisit England. I wish we had listened more closely to you when you tried to explain. I feel quite responsible that Thomas never regained happiness when he returned to his homeland and thus ended his life so tragically. Did you know that we had encouraged him to go back and visit, hoping he would benefit from a holiday?

But that is all in the past, Amelia, and now you must understand why I write this, perhaps my final letter. I want you to know that I truly understand your dilemma, your marriage difficulties, and your attraction to Jacob. For you are one of his kind and have an affinity with the blacks that no amount of Catholic education or paternal reprimands could eradicate. It is only now, in my later years, that I have come to accept our difference and to admire your patient, tolerant nature, your love of life and this country, and the freedom you allow your daughters.

The letter seemed unfinished somehow, and when her children returned, laden with closing-time goodies from a generous baker who knew their grandmother, Jackie suggested they all eat and search at the same time. Jackie was aware that her sister was watching her closely, so she laughed, making a joke of her aunt's reasoning.

"One of his kind? What is Flo saying? That because our mum had an Aboriginal father she was naturally attracted to dark-skinned people? I wonder how she explained her own mother's affair with that handsome, young Aboriginal who came calling only when Grandfather was away. I have to keep reminding myself that things were different in those days."

"Mum. Mum. Look at this." Jackie eagerly snatched the worn photograph offered by her daughter and immediately recognised her mother standing arm in arm with Jacob, a curly-haired toddler at their feet. Inscribed on the back in faded ink were the words "For my Dearest Amelia and our beautiful daughter Jacqueline."

"Our beautiful daughter, Jacqueline. Me. that's me." Jackie stood silent for a moment, examining the photo by the window light. Slowly, she raised her head and stared at her sister.

"Did you know this? Why was I not told? No wonder I didn't get on well with Dad and—oh shit—that's why he left Mum, because of me. No, because of Jacob. There must be some more to this letter somewhere."

"Jackie, nobody told me any of this, but I suppose I knew anyway." Sonia linked her arm consolingly through her sisters, and they examined the photograph together. "I just didn't want to say anything in case I was wrong. I think Dad was depressed long before you were born, and that is the reason Mum turned back to Jacob, not the other way around. She did try to make Dad happy, but people didn't understand mental illnesses back then."

Jackie could see that her own confusion was worrying her daughters, who were accustomed to her usually honest and straightforward conversations. But it did not take long for her to regain composure.

"OK, kids. This is all just a bit much to take in so quickly. Let's call it a day, and we'll finish up tomorrow." Jackie ushered her daughters out into the chilly evening and closed the door temporarily on her mother's long-neglected hoardings.

The drive home had seemed tense, as Jackie remained unusually silent. At the house, Sonia and the girls kept their thoughts to themselves as they busied themselves with the evening chores. Dinner was a simple affair with omelettes and freshly picked salad vegetables from Jackie's garden, topped off with the remaining buns and slices from Amelia's friendly baker. The family began to relax as the effects of a good meal eased their tensions.

"This explains everything, why we are so different from you and your boys, Sonia. I suppose I really knew the truth anyway, but this letter and photograph makes it real, and I am just a bit angry that Mum kept it all hidden." Jackie poured herself a glass of sparkling wine, offering the bottle to Sonia and her almost adult daughters.

"Jacob was my dad, and he was Mum's lover … forever! He never married you know, although I have heard there were other women. It's really kind of romantic, and even a little sad. How long after Mum's death was it before he also died? A year maybe, and we hardly ever visited him at the old people's home."

Jackie put her arms around her daughters and grinned suddenly. "Look at my brown-eyed girls. Just like their grandfather, eh Sonia? We've got a lot of history to catch up on tomorrow, and who knows how many more secrets we might unearth?"

Sonia managed a relieved smile as her sister and nieces so easily and excitedly accepted their heritage. Jackie poured another glass of celebratory wine and raised a toast to their discovery.

"And to think I always believed my ancestors were migrants!"

Jacob

Situated in the V where the two creeks converge lies a cottage of indeterminate vintage, now hidden behind prickly pear and banksia rose gone feral. Seasons have changed, and the creeks have been waterless for several years, drying up completely after the old man moved out. The house is still intact, but the curtains at the window are faded and torn, the front steps overgrown with rampant couch grass, and vandals have taken most of the picket fence. A battered letterbox lies on its side amongst the weeds, its name and address still visible in red paint: "Jacob Ahmad Lot 4 Brandy Creek Lane."

I remember Jacob as an elegant man, despite the mane of snowy hair falling past his shoulders at the same level as his slightly darker beard. His shoes were always polished and his trousers pressed, he walked tall and straight with the feigned aid of a heavy, carved cane, and his deep voice commanded immediate attention. Jacob carried his colour with a haughtiness that impressed, although few knew his background and he kept his past to himself. After Amelia died, he had a fall and could no longer look after himself. Mind you, there were quite a few women who were willing to help him stay at home, but he chose to leave the cottage and move to where there was constant care and companionship.

He died alone, though not lonely, at the nursing home near the old winery where he had worked for many years. The grapevines have long gone, and the old warehouse was destroyed by fire, but the remaining offices and sheds have been turned into workshops for artists and craft groups. Our local heritage society holds meetings there, and friendship groups stop in at the little café for morning tea and scones on a regular basis. It was Jacob who had fought to reopen the buildings for public use after the winery closed.

The heritage society has taken on the task of cleaning out Jacob's cottage. It had been left to Amelia, and although she passed away before him, for some reason he never rewrote his will. It took a year or two for all the red tape to be cleared before Amelia's girls could put the cottage on the market, and that would have been around the time that Jackie told us she was his daughter. When you consider his usually meticulous bookkeeping, it came as a surprise that Jacob's legal and personal affairs required organizing.

The new owners will be moving in soon, and Jackie asked us to collect anything that might be of value to the society. I joined the group at their last meeting when boxes of items from the house were to be collated and recorded. Jacob had been a hoarder of history, but our job was relatively easy because of his neatness and methodical labelling. However, it was also difficult in that we felt as though we were intruding on a personal life that had been kept so private.

I was fortunate to be given two heavy, timber boxes to examine. Borers had invaded the wood on one box, but the other was intact, its rusted latch chain hanging loosely across a label that read simply, "Cameleers." Inside, four separate compartments held wooden and metal items that I could not immediately recognise, and there was a sliding tray where Jacob had stored related paperwork. Looking closer I realised these were harnesses, tools, and papers relating to the camel trade. Carved nose pegs, metal bells, and forged hobbles shared space with huge sewing needles, buckles, and punches. In the tray there were browned and brittle photographs of turbaned men and their camels, pages of decorative Urdu script, and Jacob's own brief documentation about the articles. He had added a brief comment on how he came to inherit them from his father, an Afghan cameleer working in the Australian outback.

This was an unexpected history. I doubt now that Jacob had deliberately misled people over the years; he just never corrected them when they presumed he was of British Indian descent. Some members of our society were a little peeved that he had not told the truth, but I doubt if any of them had bothered to ask about his family, preferring to accept what they had heard. In this town, privacy is respected, and the older folk don't ask too many questions. They simply wait to be told.

The discovery had made me curious about his mother, so I finished up the day's sorting and stopped in at the cottage on the way home, hoping to find out more about Jacob's family. The door was unlocked, and a few small, dusty boxes remained in the hallway. I loaded them into the car and went back for a final look, opening cupboards and running my hand over high shelves where I could not see the top. A spider crawled softly down my arm, causing me to pull my hand away suddenly and knock a thin package, in its shroud of cobwebs, to the floor.

Dust was making me sneeze, and my eyes watered, so I closed the door on the empty house and headed to the car, eager to unwrap the parcel. I recognised the writing on the front as Jacob's, and I was hoping this would be a diary or at least something that would explain why he never spoke of his family. I carefully removed the covering and found a sheaf of handwritten notes and some faded photographs all neatly stacked and tied with string. I did feel that I was intruding on someone's privacy and considered calling Jackie, but at the same time, I was delighted to be the first one to turn the pages.

At home, I examined the notes more closely, gently separating the sections where moisture had penetrated, sticking the corners and smudging Jacob's perfect handwriting. Several pages were devoted to recollections of his parents and his limited knowledge of his mother's past. Jacob wrote that his father had been one of the last Muslim cameleers brought out from Afghanistan in the early 1900s on a three-year cartage contract. Apparently, he was one of the few who had stayed after the contract expired, continuing to work his own camels in the dry country of central Australia. Some of those migrants, his father included, were lonely for companionship and happily integrated with Aboriginal communities. He married a desert woman, perhaps not officially, but the partnership was strong according to Jacob's memories and the stories his father told him in later years.

Two babies were born to the couple early in their relationship. The young family travelled south when Aboriginal children were being taken from their parents' arms, but the move proved disastrous as the siblings succumbed to an influenza epidemic that swept across Victoria.

Jacob was born shortly after the tragedy, and the little family moved from town to town wherever there was work with horses, a step down for Jacob's father, but nonetheless lucrative. Jacob was still a youngster when his mother died, and he was raised by his father, travelling across the south-eastern states for several years. The wooden boxes went with them until father and son eventually settled in this town, in the cottage by the creeks. It was there that the boxes were stored, holding their secrets until after Jacob died.

A small photograph drifted to the floor as I lifted the next sheet. It showed a tall man in tunic and loose pants standing in front of a building formed from logs and what I presumed was packed earth. A more modern addition had been added at the side of the building, and several camels were tethered farther out the back. I turned the photograph over and read a simple inscription that said, "Father at the mosque."

For a while, I just sat thinking, and gradually I began to understand Jacob's secrets. Further readings clarified some of his feelings and even, surprisingly, his shame. Jacob's father abandoned his religion after starting a relationship with Jacob's mother and raised his son without clear spiritual instruction. According to Jacob's recollections, however, there were frequent referrals to the punishment of sin, by what or whom he did not understand.

It was only after Jacob became friends with Amelia that he turned to the Catholic Church for guidance and hoped to ease the guilt of illegitimacy and unidentified wrongdoing. Instead, he faced rejection and criticism from the local priest because he refused baptism, citing his father's Muslim religion and his mother's spiritual culture as reasons to remain uninitiated. I wondered, if the church knew of his parentage, how did Jacob keep his secrets from the rest of the townsfolk? And despite his own beliefs about illegitimacy and adultery, he had a lifelong affair with Amelia, fathering a beautiful daughter.

All I could think was that Jacob's guilt had given him the strength to devote his life to the town, appearing as a righteous citizen and doing his best to make up for what he considered past sins. He became well respected within the business community and Amelia's name was never tarnished. Again, I had to remind myself that Jacob and Amelia had managed to keep their affair private, at least until after her husband's suicide. He would not have wanted to start rumours about mixed race children, as that had been the fearful reason for his own parents moving farther south. Things were different in those days.

The last few pages appeared to contain the beginnings of a diary written after Jackie's birth. I was tempted to continue reading, but my conscience and the dust got the better of me, so I put the package aside. This was Jackie's father, and I believe the information contained in those personal notes belonged only to her. I might never understand the true depth of Jacob's self-imposed shame, but my curiosity had been gratified and my respect for him ameliorated.

Ginny and Rose

There's a large, round clock in the food court, and if I focus on it for a while, the hands become clear enough for me to read. I often sit there filling in time before I have to catch the bus from the train station. "Blind Betty" they call me nowadays. I count the steps, and my stick helps me find the way. Couldn't do without my stick, so when I overheard that gentleman talking to his lady friend about Jacob's walking cane, my ears pricked up, and I have to admit I listened carefully to the rest of the conversation.

You see I knew Jacob well when we were younger and even went to a few dances with him. He was a very handsome man, but his heart belonged to Amelia and no one else stood a chance. I remember the cane with all its intricate carvings because it always sat just inside the front door of his cottage. His father had made it from a piece of timber he found in the scrub somewhere in West Australia. It has a history, that old stick, and Jacob would have liked to know that it is still being used.

While I waited and listened, two young children ran up and hugged the gentleman quickly, then returned to their mother, calling out their goodbyes as they ran. He explained their presence to his friend, who made some comment about their dark skin that I did not quite hear and that he obviously felt deserved more clarification.

> They are my grandchildren, those two, Ginny and Rose, nearly six, and I still can't tell the difference. Good kids, both of them. Live down there by the creek. Their mum and dad,

my daughter Jess and her partner Ben, bought that old fella's place, you know, that tall black guy who died a coupla years back? Oh, what was his name? Some biblical thing like Joseph, James—oh yes. It was Jacob. Jacob.

Ginny came home from school the other day, all red-eyed and sobbing quietly. Apparently, they'd had show-and-tell or whatever and Ginny took that old, carved, walking stick—Jacob had left it in the house and the kids fancied it when the agent was showing them through. They just walked out to the car with it, and my daughter was too embarrassed to take it back. Anyway, I think she wanted to keep it, with all those carvings and that rich, red wood.

Well, as I said, she had shown it in class, and later on, a couple of the boys started teasing her in the playground. Apparently, Jess had explained to the girls that it belonged to an Aboriginal and that he had found the stick in the bush, made all the pictures, and he was black. Ginny didn't even blink an eye, but those other kids brought it all home.

You see, her daddy has Aboriginal ancestors, way back, and he tells the twins stories about them all the time. So Ginny added that information to her talk session. Didn't think anything of it at the time except that it was something that made her family interesting, exotic I suppose, although she wouldn't know that word. You saw their dark eyes and that mop of curly, black hair that are obviously a throwback on her dad's side.

That's OK with us, of course, but out in the playground, they really copped it all, and those bullies haven't let up since. The twins get called all kinds of names now. Maybe Ben and Jess shouldn't have told them about their ancestors after all, just kept it quiet. You think you are doing the right thing by giving

> them a history to be proud of, but then it backfires and the kids suffer.
> Little Rose, the quiet one of the two, brought me the walking stick just this morning and asked me to keep it because it made them unhappy She hasn't learned yet what racism is all about and just associated the stick with the name-calling.

I had to interrupt their conversation then to clear up a few points and offer a suggestion or two. I explained that the stick had belonged to Jacob's father who was an Afghan cameleer, not an Aboriginal. I said that perhaps the children could avoid the bullying if they had another talk session describing how those Afghans helped open up the Australian outback with their desert skills and their camels. They had great courage, and our old timers could not have managed without them.

As an afterthought, I added that, in my opinion, nobody should mention that the Afghans were Muslims. The children should only be burdened with one problem at a time.

Johnny Tarawa

You like this house? It was built by Johnny Tarawa back thirty, forty years ago. He was an architect. Built it himself, with the help of his wife, from the ground up. Used all the stones from the creek to make the walls in the main part. Made mud bricks for the rest and even had some of the timber from the property treated for the internal beams.

He was way ahead of his time, even though the locals thought he was mad, with all his money, to do that hard work without the help of tradies. He's semi-retired now. That's why I was able to buy the place. He still does some designing for people who ask, but usually he spends his time volunteering. Helps the Indigenous folk, mostly teaching them art and design. Gets them started on courses at the TAFE. Guess you would call him a kind of mentor.

He's a real artist, that guy. Very clever with his paint and his woodcarving. Come inside and I'll show you what I mean. Come through here, and turn around. He painted the back of this door, by hand, with individual dots. Must have taken months to finish, and he said he just designed it as he went along. This is the lounge room. Takes your breath away, doesn't it? Look at that mural above the fireplace. Colours of the desert make you feel like you are really out there. And if you look closely, you can see little lizards and marsupials hidden amongst the rocks and sand. Over there, see how he has carved boomerangs, talking sticks, faces and handprints into the corner posts and uprights, along with a few serpents and even that croc on the ceiling beam.

Should be opened as a museum, but he didn't want all that publicity and stuff. Sold it to me on condition that I only let friends visit, not have heaps of tourists wandering through the place. I had to sign a paper, a kind of unofficial caveat, promising that none of his artwork would be destroyed in his lifetime or opened to the public.

Keep coming. There's more. This is the kitchen where he painted while his wife cooked. She died a couple of years back, so he had to cover her portrait for a while. He says I can remove the plywood and show her face at the end of the year. It's something to do with Indigenous culture and avoiding images of the deceased.

Oh, didn't I mention it? Johnny Tarawa is an Aboriginal, an elder now, I believe. I know he's not black and his parents are white, but they adopted him when he was just a baby. When he was building this house, he said he started to look into different earthy colours and was attracted to the desert paintings in caves and overhangs of northern Australia. His father, who was ill at the time and died not long after, noticed Johnny's attraction to Aboriginal culture and decided to tell him the truth about his background.

You see, even though he was aware that he was adopted, all his life Johnny Tarawa had presumed his birthparents were white. His real father apparently was, but his mother was an Aboriginal from some mob up north. He said it was kind of a relief to know because he had always felt a difference that he couldn't quite put his finger on.

When he found out, he changed his life completely. Started looking up his family tree and learning all about his aunts and uncles, cousins and the whole caboodle. He had no children of his own, so he began helping out kids who were in trouble. Financially as well as emotionally, you know. Put them all on to this wall here in the hallway, although he said he wasn't allowed to add their names.

Over the years, he just added more paintings, mostly about people he knew or incidents that happened. This one here on the toilet door is about an argument over the grasslands along the railway track. He was pretty much a greenie back then. He might have mellowed a little, but you wouldn't want to argue against him when it comes to the environment or Aboriginal culture or racism and stuff.

Here, come through here to the bedroom. That mural was the last one he painted. It's the story of his life, right from his beginnings in the desert country up until the death of his wife. You can see how the colours flow from the rich ochres of his childhood through to the sombre greys of his youth and here, where he discovered his heritage, the brilliant blues and greens of a renewed life. Brings out the poet in you, doesn't it? Along with memories you didn't even know you had.

How can I live with all this? Oh, it's not difficult. You see, I'm one of those guys on the wall in the hallway.

Little Fox

He was later than usual this Saturday morning. Others had gone up before him, and he did not want to get close. He stopped at the foot of Mount Lion and pulled a drink from his pack, resting his back against the cold, basalt outcrop as he looked down Reserve Road towards the town. The tips of his fingers whitened against the canteen when he turned his head slightly, noting the position of the intruders.

OK, it's a public place. Mount Holden. Mount Lion. Disrupted my day. That's all.

He wasn't around when local kids gradually changed the name, somehow turning the Holden emblem into the lion of the hill.

Nobody has bothered to find out its real name. Not even a mountain really. Just an old hill losing a bit more height each year.

He doesn't remember when there were only a few houses evolving from the dust and onion weed. Occasional heavy rains eroded muddy channels connecting the hill to the flats and dumping layers of fine silt into Jack's Creek at the northern edge of the town. His mum took a commission shack there and gathered his siblings from the paddocks each night, packing them warmly into the two, yellowed bedrooms. They were almost grown when he was born, lighter than the others but with the same dark pools for eyes.

Whitey, he called me. Why did he come back?

Towards the south, he could see a watcher silhouetted in his window. The old man had cursed the youths that spat on his polished mailbox as they passed towards the hill in the early morning. His day would be spent, as usual, washing the dust off his garden, turning the hose in quiet anger on passing cars that churned the fine white clay of the road into clouds of talcum. He watched the boy in his earth-coloured clothes make his pilgrimage away from the town and waited for the return, remembering his own days of youthful searching. The boy did not turn, but he understood.

Did he know my mother, once?

Soon the road will be built. Then the hose will be put away, and the boy will find a new route away from and into reality. The old man's waiting might seem longer, meaningless.

Nothing will really change.

If you sit in the right spot at the top, you can see 360 degrees. Mount Macedon in the west, blue green and hazy, stealing the rains before they reach Mount Lion. The south, hung with a brown veil by day, glows with city lights at night. The boy prefers to turn his back to the lights and watch the northern sky hanging darkly over the dry and treeless plains that have so far resisted development.

Sometimes, he stands on the eastern edge and frowns at the town beetling around below.

They're closing in. Coming closer. What's the point of it all? They move in to our little town to feel the country and then cry for progress, stuff to make it like the city they left behind. People doing nothing, being nothing, want more, so they can go on doing the same. That's their reality, not mine.

Few people go to the hilltop. Some say they've seen evidence of a night camp in one of the shallow wind-worn caves.

Leave stuff here so they think I spend the night in this hole. Leave nothing but leaves in the other. I am the lion of the hill.

He knew they followed him that morning, from a distance, using binoculars. They were already on the hill, just below the summit, waiting, watching him coming. They saw him climb the rocky outcrop on the eastern edge and then wend his way between the tussocks of introduced spear grass and the purple globes of Scotch thistle. Slowly, slowly.

I'm really the only one who should be here.

As they watched, he sank to his knees, pulling the sharp-toothed grass seeds from his trouser legs. They turned to each other, and in that instant, he was gone. No grass moved. Nothing. The youths waited, puzzled and wary. After a time, they edged their way down to where he had vanished, searching the hollows and lichen-crusted rocks, before returning to their original vantage spot. There they sat, quietly eating chips and Coke, chucking the empties into the tawny undergrowth.

He couldn't have passed them—they would have seen him. What was he up to? Did he know they were watching? Startled by a movement from above, they turned to see him rise from the grass and continue his climb, apparently unaware of their presence.

Why have they come? They think I don't know. They think I haven't seen them before, spying on me. They will follow my trail, come closer to find, curious, like the little roos hiding behind the bracken.

He entered the cave, making sure the watchers saw him, and then peered out at them from a corner, his black eyes reflecting no light. The sun was almost west and shone on the lank figures coming closer across the pitted hilltop. He knew their line of vision would be blocked by gorse and they would have to come around by the left to avoid the savage thorns.

Quick, quick. Scuttle, scuttle, little fox. I'll do you proud, Mum. Down on all fours, under the bed, the cupboard, before he sees. Out the side of the cave and across its roof. They'll think I'm still inside. A trapped rabbit. A cunning fox.

He sat still waiting, waiting.

They're in. Run on silent feet, faster, faster. Push the grate down through the opening, and ram it hard into the red earth. Quick, quick, jam in the beam and melt into the night, away until their voices are muffled like foxes whimpering in snares.

He had learned from his mother how to make a fire with little smoke, but he preferred to wait until dark, keeping the flames low so as not to be noticed from the town. In the amber light, he crushed red scoria on the harder rocks and mixed the powder with water from his canteen. From his pack, he took out a small container of white clay collected from the lower slopes across from the watcher's house and stirred it into a paste. With his finger, he dragged lines, first of one colour, then another, across from the bridge of his nose and down across cheeks darkened by the sun. On his chin, he dabbed spots, one for each of his brothers and smaller ones for the sisters he never really knew.

Why didn't you stop him? You shouldn't have cut out and left us alone with him.

The night wind comes up here from the west, dragging at the bracken and rushes and dropping its residue at the eastern mouth of his cave before whooshing down across the town in gusty swells and dust clouds. He had set the trail well, but the wind would have swept it clean by morning.

You taught me well, Mum. Those stories. How to hide. How to keep silent. How his bones would rot in the scoria and the little ferns would grow green around them. It wasn't easy bringing them here, but it was harder living there. They thought he'd left us like the first time. They didn't really care.

Sometimes as he slept, he dreamed of the spirits that had heaved the great basalt blocks from the plains below and packed them between with gritty, red scoria. They fought with the wind that whipped through the cracks and swirled the pebbles into widening circles, hollowing caves to shelter the wallabies that even now bounded up, away from the new estates and marauding dogs.

He slept easily, pulling his blanket close around his shoulders and tucking it under his chin to keep snakes from sliding into his clothes.

As a cold, pale mist drifted up from the southern slope and dissipated with the rising sun, he stretched in his hide and listened for a time to the skylarks calling in the day. Gently, he stroked the bluetongue that had crawled close to his warmth and watched as it slithered from the rocks into a shaft of sunlight.

He listened. He could hear what he wanted to hear, apart from the birds. Silence. He slid into the light on his belly, rested, and then crawled through the spaces between the tussocks. From behind the cave, he could see no movement. He put his ear to the ground and heard the thump of boots against the metal grate.

My feet were too small, Mum. I couldn't open the cupboard with them, but it didn't matter. After a while, I liked the dark where he couldn't get me. You always came when he'd gone.

Sunday evening. This day, he ignored the road and came down through the paddocks across from the new houses framed with white roses and arum lilies. He liked their outer orderliness but did not want to pass into their interior.

It's my last time. I won't be back. They've taken my freedom and pushed me farther out. That's what they've done to us.

He hesitated at the clearing where dancing feet had long ago carved rings on the hillside. As he crossed the first circle, he felt the spirits rise, lightening his feet and swirling inside his head. The old man sat at his window and waited. A smile teetered momentarily beneath the scowl as he watched the boy dance silently across the ancient furrows.

Tjala

Carefully, methodically, the artist dips her stick into the old jam jar of yellow ochre, returning again and again to the canvas with a silent patience, mapping her spirit stories in lines of dotted colour.

Tjala is an out-of-date hippie. She walks with music at her side in the form of little silver bells, tangled amongst floating earth-coloured ribbons attached to a pale, driftwood walking staff. Her multi-layered, rainbow-hued skirts brush against ankles encased in worn, purple Doc Martins. She buys her rough, woven jackets and fringed shawls from Cosmic Clothing in the centre of town and beads her own hair once or twice a year, careless of the greying wisps that escape and fringe her weathered, brown face.

In her sunroom studio, there is no furniture. A paint-splattered awning fragment laid on the floor serves as her workbench. Three sides of this awning are pinned down with jars and battered tins containing her tools. Frayed sticks in various thicknesses, brushes and feathers, and erasers and rags sit in their containers alongside notebooks and pencils. The fourth side is where Tjala sits on her floor cushions with easy access to the canvas. From there, she can watch the crimson rosellas in the bush reserve behind her house and smell the eucalypts on a rainy morning. Along the studio walls, there are perhaps a hundred finished paintings leaning against each other with only their plywood skeletons visible to guests. Not that there are many guests invited to this part of the house.

For the most part, Tjala lives without people, sharing her house with two or three large, coloured rats and a cockatiel that scolds the rodents constantly from his perch above the kitchen window. The painting she works on has no people, no animals, and no plants. It is of the desert sands, the harsh sun, and dried riverbeds that might have held water many centuries past. She mixes her colours on a piece of paperbark already heavy with thick pools of yellow and orange acrylic.

Occasionally, she must sell some paintings in order to live, to pay bills and feed her companions. The canvases are carefully bubble wrapped and sent by air to a gallery in Darwin where they are sold to international tourists. Her signature is the painting itself, not a name scrawled in a corner demanding attention or bringing rejection.

Someone from the local newspaper once called to inquire about her art, asking whether it was ethically correct to pretend her work was authentic, sourced in the desert far from this cool, green landscape. Tjala politely showed her into the kitchen where some of the paintings hung, laying family photographs face down as she moved through the rooms and offering no explanation. The rats appeared, probably curious about the newcomer and the office smells she brought with her. Tjala never bothered to show her the studio, and she left without a story.

Finishing the dots, the artist takes a crumpled tube of deep orange and empties most of it in the centre of the canvas. She takes a strong, black feather and moves the colour outwards in radiating waves of burning sunshine. Kool n Deadly radio plays country music, and she occasionally sings along, the feather temporarily suspended above the orange sun as she moves her shoulders to the rhythm.

Tjala pays little heed to the thin wisps of smoke coming from the lean-to on the other side of her back fence. She knows that youths often shelter there in the reserve, smoking after school, and she turns the radio louder to drown out their cursing.

At day's end, the artist lights the fire and sits back down to lay the finishing touches. Deep bands of yellow dots glow in the flickering light and blend into the darker stained lines of her memories. She writes, "Papunya Dreaming," in her notebook, where the paintings are listed and numbered. She listens to songs about brown-skinned babies being taken away, about deaths in custody, and troubled youths searching for understanding.

Tjala wipes away the tears before they spoil her work.

Harmony

Harmony dropped another note in the mailbox, the third in as many weeks. The woman had seemed so nice over the phone, helpful and understanding, inviting her to the meetings held sometimes at the little coffee shop in the alley. Now she hadn't answered the emails or responded to Harmony knocking on the door.

Had they become aware of her background, of the violence long gone, of her part in the violence, her anger and her betrayals? Surely, they could understand that this was the reason she wanted their company, their conversations and support. And wasn't kinship what the meetings were about?

Winter evenings darkened early. Harmony wandered slowly home, the icy wind a relief after the stuffy train. She passed by the closed café, its dimmed interior lights casting a warm, brown glow onto the leafy footpath. Harmony pressed her face to the window, gloved hands cupping her eyes in order to see into the back where Ian sometimes worked late, sorting the bush tucker teas and wattle seed biscuits for tomorrow's trendy do-gooders. The alternative life in a country town enticed these newcomers, so now they inhabit the alleys and cafes that exhale coffee fumes to remind them of the crowded places they have left behind in Melbourne. They buy their handmade scarves and hats, their country-style pickles and jams and doughy breads, organic nuts and recycled books from the local craft markets, and carry their booty into sculptured spec homes in estates that are eating up the good land, the market gardens, and the silt beds along the creek banks. They sign petitions to fill in the mosquito-infested watercourses now devoid of frogs and poisoned by detergents pumped from grey water pits.

Harmony had protested loudly. She soon learned how to sit carefully, so as not to be thrown around inside the divvy vans. Locked up, she continued to protest, dealing out her own racial taunts to those she believed discriminated against her because of her colour. Nobody visited her, although the guy from Legal Aid was OK. At least, he listened when she told how the fat councillor had got in her way, how she broke his nose, and how he swore he had never cared if she was black or white, but she didn't believe him anyway. Now Harmony was the first to admit that her own prejudiced anger had no real basis except that which she had imagined. She had to fill out those forms that asked if she was Aboriginal or of Torres Strait Islander descent, as if they couldn't tell. Harmony wrote no, because she did not want special treatment.

Whatever that entailed.

It wasn't being locked up that set her back; it was the community-based orders that the judge recommended. And him being black himself, she thought he'd understand. There were months on and off of graffiti removal, and if you missed the bus from the pick-up centre, you were done for; the order extended and the court costs piled on. Three years it took altogether, and it wasn't until her late twenties that Harmony began slowly to find an inner peace.

A stinging rain was settling in across the empty streets as she tried to shake those bad memories and think about how things seemed to have changed. How she'd gone back to school, did a few weeks here and there of courses that fizzled until Ian put her onto the agency. Temping in the city made it easier for her to work, knowing that each week there would be different faces, different feelings, and she would not have time to stir up trouble or argue her case before moving on to the next job.

The city was impersonal, the constant stream of faces familiar only because of their consistency. She did not need to know them and was able to hide amongst the unsmiling crowds with their dark suits and hurrying manner, using her lunch hours to sit alone and write letters of protest or listen to Indigenous radio.

Harmony realised now that her own discrepancies had been what made her equal to those she had sought to harm. Ian had been encouraging and said she had to be better than them, had to learn how to fight them quietly with words. If only she could contact those people, join a group where those like her feel comfortable. But the group wanted members who were whitewashed, not someone who would tarnish their image as passive, tolerant, and proud. They wanted people who had been wronged, not those who had done wrong for whatever reason. All she needed was time to talk and show them that the land, once belonging to their ancestors before the Clarkes and Evans and Jacksons moved them out, had been inhabited by wildlife that had now disappeared from the waterways and remnant box-eucalypt forests. The hills and the plains had once been productive, and now only a few acres of native grassland remained, protected fiercely by a committee that fought against those who demanded more shops, more car parks, and plastic playgrounds.

But that same committee feared her reasons for joining. Did they think that because of her ancestral rights she was going to claim the land as her own? Harmony was learning to voice her opinions quietly, through the local newspapers and heritage groups where her colour would not be seen, but still her reputation was held against her and the Indigenous meetings in the café remained outside her boundaries.

It wasn't her race that turned the group against her, for she was one of them. It was their ignorance and their inability to see that the land was being destroyed by those who sought aesthetic improvements. They could not understand that her fight was not because of personal bitterness but to regain some dignity that had been lost with the land. She just needed people to see the value in keeping some of it for future regeneration and to study its uniqueness and history. Harmony truly could not understand those citizens who believed their rights took precedence over other living creatures and their habitat.

The problem was that she had been born in this area while they were newcomers, all of them. Some had come from the north, but most were from the city where they had learned to use their colour as a prop and a means of gaining respectful attention. They had been raised elsewhere, and their affinity for the land had been cultivated by the new cultural awareness developed in the schools, the media, and political forums. Harmony did not wish to criticize their intentions, but she knew their idea of belonging was different from hers. Despite their differences, she needed to speak with them as kin, and their rejection was more hurtful than the distrust from the environmental factions.

As the rain soaked through her trench coat, dripping from the hem into her long boots, Harmony climbed the back stairs to her unit. A stray kitten shivered on the doormat, its wet fur flattened against a protruding spine. She gently cradled the feral animal against her, whispering to it her thoughts on people who allowed their cats to wander, heedless of the danger to birds and animals that really belonged in this region.

A brief flash of her old temper returned as she stood under a pale light on the tiny porch. Harmony unlocked the door, bending down to place the kitten inside before reaching in and turning on the interior lamp. She did not enter, instead telling the kitten she would be back soon. She closed the door and hurried down the rain-blackened steps.

It was still early. She would catch that woman at her evening meal and put her foot in the door if necessary. Harmony retraced her steps, hurrying against the cold that was beginning to penetrate her damp coat and whip wet strands of hair against her cheeks. As she walked, she rehearsed a speech, choosing her words carefully and giving priority to the important issues. How could she explain to that woman the connection between the local environment and the Indigenous community? How could she explain that if the group added their voice to the protests something might get done?

Harmony felt alone in this town. Her parents and siblings have moved on, moved out as the city people drifted in, bringing their shopping malls and electric trains, their graffiti and vandalism, their cries for more infrastructures to cope with their growing families and car numbers. She needed the group for support in standing against the land grabs, but more importantly, she needed their kinship, their friendship.

Or did she? Stopping suddenly just metres from the house, Harmony stood in the rain, straightening her shoulders and wiping the drips from her face. She had never needed people before, so why now? Struggling against momentary confusion and doubt, she did not know whether to turn back or to knock on the door. She had to sort out her real reasons for being there.

Determined then, Harmony walked the last few paces and peered through the mailbox opening. Her note was still there, sharing space with coloured advertising brochures and community newspapers. She knocked loudly on the door and waited for an answer, a speech clear in her mind about local knowledge and progress, about coming together and standing against the disbelievers.

She would not back down this time, for she knew that they needed her.

Aunty May's Group

No one came when she knocked the first time. "I know you are there," she mumbled to herself. "Once more then I'll go."

Harmony rang the doorbell with one hand and knocked loudly on the glass insert with the other. A woman in her late fifties finally answered, holding the door only slightly open, either keeping back the cold air or afraid of the caller. Harmony offered her hand in greeting through the slit and the woman took it softly, cautiously.

"I'm Harmony. I called you about the meetings a few weeks ago, and I've left you notes that you haven't answered. That's OK though, because I understand you are a busy woman, but I really need to talk to you."

"Oh yes, I'm Aunty May. You had better come in out of the rain. I'll get you a towel."

"I won't stay long. I found a kitten in the rain and shoved it in my door. I had better get home to give it some food and warm it up." Not at all like the speech she had rehearsed.

Aunty May looked at Harmony, her head tilted quizzically to one side.

"What?" Harmony questioned the woman.

"Oh. It's just that … Well, I have heard some things about your behaviour, and it surprises me that you would take in a stray kitten. No offence meant, you understand?"

"None taken," Harmony replied, although the comment cut deeply, and her fingernails bit into her palms. Holding back on the usual reaction, she accepted the towel, wiping her hands and face, fluffing her bedraggled hair, and then reaching down to wipe her boots. She handed the towel back to Aunty May, apologising for the dirty black streaks marring its whiteness. Ian had been right in telling her that there were quieter ways to vent her feelings, but she knew this was not a good start to the evening.

Aunty May led her through the house into the warm kitchen where three other people sat sipping aromatic herbal tea. The remains of an early meal lay on the sink where used plates were stacked neatly and food scraps filled a large bowl. Harmony made a mental note to ask for some of the scraps to feed her kitten, if the evening went well.

"Harmony, this is Uncle Will, Greg, and Lisa. They all belong to our Indigenous group, and we've been discussing the last morning meeting that we held down at the café. It seems our group is getting smaller, Harmony, and that is one of the reasons we never answered your request to join. After this week, we might not even exist. Sit down and I'll pour some tea, if you like."

Harmony felt a little guilty about blackening the towel. As usual, she had jumped to conclusions and had probably misunderstood the intentions of these people and their slackness in replying to her notes.

"Thanks, Auntie May. I'll have peppermint, if that's OK. I could smell it as I came through the door."

Will's gnarled brown hands gripped his mug of steaming dark tea, the short-chipped nails and calloused knuckles indicative of work outdoors. She recognized his wrinkled face from newspaper articles, dealing with farms on the southern side of town being cut up for new freeways and industrial estates, although she couldn't quite remember his viewpoint on the matter. Surely, he would understand her drive for some kind of compromise in using land that should be saved as a green belt around the town or alternative farming for future generations.

As an Aboriginal elder, Will had the right to speak first, and he addressed her in a quiet, carefully moderated tone while he added several spoonfuls of sugar to his brew.

"You see, Harmony, we are really only a kinship group. We are just friends with a common background, and most of the Indigenous folk around here are too interested in more exciting social outings to take much notice of us.

Our main purpose is mateship, and that's something people don't seem to be interested in these days."

"But Uncle Will, with due respect, there are so many important issues that could benefit from your backing and that in turn would bring in more members. Mateship can still exist, even become stronger when people fight for a cause like their own dignity or the environment or social justice." Harmony had to pull herself up before she turned them against her. She needed to have patience, testing their welcome and looking for a suitable opening in the conversation to voice her opinions. Patience, however, was never her virtue.

"What are you all hiding from? Are you afraid that if you say what you really think you'll be rejected, ostracized by white people, by your neighbours, and maybe even lose some friends? What kind of friends are they anyway if they don't speak to you just because you have different ideas than them? Or is it just that you have no interest in this town?"

The damage was done. No turning back now.

"I've lived here all my life, except on the occasions when I've been locked up, but you already know about that, I'm sure. I have seen how building, removal of soil, inadequate drainage, removal of trees, filling in the creeks, poisoning roadside vegetation—heaps of stuff in the name of progress—have just turned this town into an unsustainable suburban dump."

Harmony stopped suddenly, aware that they were all looking at her silently, frowning over their mugs of tea.

"Sorry, I take that back. I should have said sustainable dump, unsustainable progress."

Harmony waited for a response, the long seconds making her uneasy. Greg and Lisa both spoke up together. Harmony hoped Lisa would continue, as she was younger than the others and might understand the need for action a little more, but she handed over to Greg.

"OK, girl, what is it you really want from us?" His voice was deep and gravelly, and it struck Harmony as odd that this rugged-looking, middle-aged man in his checked scum shirt enjoyed herbal tea. He obviously cared little about how he was rated and might just be the ally she needed.

"Look, it's not really that much. I feel that I am too alone in everything I do to keep this town rural, you know, not so much a suburb of Melbourne. There are other groups and individuals who have their say, but we don't seem to be on the same level. The Heritage Society and Grasslands Committee are afraid that, as an Indigenous person, I must have an ulterior motive. While they haven't been nasty to me, they certainly haven't welcomed my suggestions, and I never receive their newsletters or notifications about meetings. It's not as though I haven't asked."

"Well, let's be honest, girl. You have got yourself a reputation in this town for troublemaking. We've been a bit hesitant ourselves because we know we can't afford to antagonize anyone." Greg laughed and proceeded to relate the story about a certain gentleman and his broken nose.

Harmony was not laughing. Icily, she interrupted the joke. "Greg, this is important to me, and you'll see it is important to the future of this place. Our people have a history here, but that is not the only thing that matters. There's this concreter that I know. He says that if the excavators unearth any bones or artefacts, they just bury them again quickly, before anybody notices. You see, they lose money if there is a delay, so they make sure none of the crazies around town hear about it."

"Crazies? Does that mean us?" Finally, Lisa had spoken and Harmony hurried to explain. Things were not going as well as she had wanted.

"No, no, Lisa. You misunderstand what I am saying. That's just what the concreters and other tradies call the greenies and heritage groups. What I am trying to say is that this spate of building, endorsed by governments, not only impacts on the land and the wildlife but on our own unexplored history. Once the houses and factories are built, there's no hope of going back. We need to slow them down and make sure all the necessary studies have been done. Do you see what I am after?"

"Not really." Uncle Will got up from the table, taking the mugs and returning with a plate of cheese and dry biscuits. "Is it the environment you want to save? Is it our history, or the town itself? Are you just up in arms about change, any kind of change? Perhaps you just enjoy being controversial. What do you really want from us?"

"Pretty simple, actually. I just need to be able to say that you are behind me, that when I speak, I represent the Indigenous community in this town. I don't have any power as an individual, but all of us together would be awesome."

"There are so few of us that I doubt we would make a difference to your protests. At the most, we have probably nine or ten members." Aunty May busied herself wiping up crumbs before continuing. "I don't see how we can help. If we do agree, you must understand that we always advocate passive protests. If we give you our backing, it would have to be something we were certain would succeed and be of benefit to our group. We don't want to stand out as rabble raisers. You must abide by our rules and respect our privacy."

"I'm not good at rules," Harmony began, then she immediately realised she had said the wrong thing and changed tack. "But if rules are what it takes to get you on my side, then rules it is."

The wall phone buzzed loudly, and May answered. She listened briefly and then called to Greg. "It's the CFA, Greg. There's a house fire, and they are short of volunteers. Not what you would expect on such a rainy night."

Greg listened for a moment then grabbed his jacket and hurried to the door, explaining as he went. "I have to go. It's the artist's place down by the reserve. Her studio is alight, but they think she's OK. Catch you guys at the next meeting. You too, Harmony."

"See you, Greg." Harmony stood to leave, pleased that she had at least been invited to the meeting and not willing to wear out her welcome at May's house. "I had better go and see to the kitten. Umhh, Auntie May, would it be OK if I took some of your meat scraps for the cat?"

Ian had been right. It was all about self-control and getting people on your side. He wasn't that bad for a white guy, and she might even take him up on the offer of a date, one day.

Sarah

"Oh my God, it's Sarah. You know Sarah from Ag College. Used to go out with Tristan, that rich guy."

Elodie pointed excitedly through the café window at a young woman seated with a group of mostly older people. Laughing, she dragged Ben through the beaded door curtain and across to the table where aromas of coffee and cake mingled with the waxy perfume exuding from shelves of handmade candles and soaps.

"Sarah, how are you? It's been such a long time. Are you living in this town now or just visiting?" She interrupted the conversation at the table without hesitation. Ben protested at her lack of tact, but Elodie had never been one to consider politeness more important than her own desires.

Sarah stood in surprise and hugged Elodie warmly. "It's so good to see you again, Elodie. You too, Ben. I'm just visiting, helping Aunty May out for a while actually."

She rested her hands on the shoulders of a dark woman colourfully attired in a printed orange caftan, with heavy jewellery on her wrists and fingers. She then proceeded to introduce all the other members of the group, touching their heads as she walked around the table.

"Greg, Uncle Will, Lisa, and her mother Lil, Thomas, Colin, and Samantha. Now this is Harmony, the newest member of our team and the main reason I've come to help out. She wants to stir up this town and save us all, but her reputation as an Indigenous troublemaker holds her back a bit."

Sarah laughed at Harmony's grimace and turned to Elodie.

"Actually, the two of you would get on quite well with your lack of respect for authority and your stubbornness when it comes to doing whatever you believe is right. I live in Melbourne now. My job involves sustainability and environment, so I can help Harmony with inside knowledge. Aunty May is in charge of Indigenous studies at the TAFE where Lisa and Lil are students, Greg is a farmer, and the others all work for the local council."

A young woman came from behind the counter and began to clear the table. The group stood, pushing out the old bentwood chairs to reveal worn carvings of kookaburras, lyrebirds, and kangaroos on the backrests. Elodie noticed the chair cushions matched the material of the tablecloth, expensive looking and exotic with dreamtime motifs and dotted circles in brilliant ochre colours.

Aunty May spoke to Sarah, and the group left, politely shaking the newcomers' hands and murmuring their goodbyes. While the group was leaving, Elodie looked around the café shop and fingered the goods for sale, admiring the clever handiwork of disabled and disadvantaged artisans from other communities.

"What is this place, Sarah? Who are those people? Is this a kind of Aboriginal meeting place? Did I interrupt something?"

Sarah laughed. "Yes, you did interrupt, but that's OK as we had finished our meeting anyway. How on earth do you put up with her, Ben?"

Elodie put her arm through Ben's and leaned happily against him. "Because he loves me." She looked up at her tall, fair-haired boyfriend, and he kissed the top of her head in agreement.

"Yeah, I guess she's OK. What about Tristan, Sarah? Are you two still an item?" Ben asked, curious about a past relationship that had seemed so perfect.

Sarah busied herself searching for something in her bag and did not look at Elodie or Ben. "No. Walk with me to the village green where we can sit in the shade, and I'll tell you all about it, if you like. I know you'd like a juicy scandal, Elodie, so this might just disappoint you. It's not very intriguing. I haven't really told anyone else, so it will do me good to get it off my chest."

"Ooh, the drama. Release all that anger, reveal your dire secrets, make out as a victim, all that stuff. Bring it on, Sarah. We are all ears." Elodie laughed teasingly.

The seats in the park were covered with bird droppings, spilled soft drinks, and fish and chip papers. Sarah picked up the rubbish, carefully opened the council bin with one finger to avoid the greasy food smears, and threw the papers inside. She wiped her hands with antiseptic cleaner, took another look at the seats, and decided to sit on the summer-dried grass, beckoning her friends to join her.

"You haven't changed much in three years, Sarah. You were my best friend yet we've hardly spoken in all that time, since uni finished. Now tell us about everything that has happened since we saw you last." Elodie lay back in the grass, resting her head on her floppy leather bag and watching the sky through the lacy branches of century-old oak trees, a legacy from the early residents of the town.

"OK, but just answer me one question, Elodie. And Ben. When we first met as teenagers at the college, did you know I was of Aboriginal descent?"

Elodie turned her head to Sarah, squinting against the sun. "Nah. I mean yes, probably. I can't remember even thinking about it, you know. Why?"

"Ben?"

"I just knew you as Sarah. I didn't even think about who you were other than as a student, same as us."

"Would it have mattered had you known?"

"God no!" Elodie and Ben chorused together, looking quizzically at Sarah.

"Well, it certainly mattered to Tristan." Sarah pulled some chocolate out of her handbag, broke it into squares, and handed it to her friends.

"We were together for about five months, and then we had to go out and do that work experience, you remember. I told Tristan that he could work on our sheep and cattle property in South Australia for a few months, and his parents offered to let me work on their stud farm up near Bright. Sounded like the perfect arrangement and we could alternate with weekends, one at his place and the other at my parents' place.

We decided to drive over to South Australia just before Christmas and make all the arrangements for a start in February. To fill in a couple of weeks between completing all the assignments and going to my place, we went to the Gold Coast. That's when things started to go a bit skew-whiff. Some of his mates were there, and they were teasing me about how brown I was becoming up there in the sun, while Tristan just got burnt. They made some snide references to me being a nigga, an abo, and stuff like that, jokingly of course, but those jokes hurt, you know.

I'll never forget the look he gave me that evening. It was as though he had never really seen me before. He should have asked them to shut up, but he just stayed silent. We forgot about it the next day, or at least I did. Thinking back though, I realise he was pretty quiet on the flight home."

"But surely, Sarah, he knew you were black. I mean, look at you." Elodie rubbed the dark skin on Sarah's arm admiringly, comparing it to her own gingery freckles and light colouring.

"If you think back, Elodie," Ben suggested, "you will remember that Tristan had only known Sarah in the cooler months when her tan had faded. She looked just like us. Well, almost. She looked just like the majority of the students down there at Ag College who worked outdoors on their farms."

Sarah laughed at Ben's attempt to ease her feelings of reject. "Are you saying I looked weatherworn, like an old farmer or something?"

"Oh, no I didn't mean it like that ..."

"It's OK, Ben. I know what you are getting at, and you are right. Tristan would not have known, and I just never thought to tell him. I suppose the opportunity never came up. He showed no interested in my family or friends anyway, and I've had plenty of time to think about what he was really like. Self-centred, that's what he was, and I am definitely better off without him."

"So, did he just dump you?" Elodie asked.

"Not right away. He came to meet my parents and arrange for all the work experience, but he was very cool towards me. Still, Tristan was polite to my folks, and we had a fairly enjoyable weekend before he left to go back to Bright. He was supposed to arrange for my visit to his farm, but instead, I got a letter in the mail saying it was all off. He said the drought had made it impossible for me to find suitable work in that area, and his parents could not justify employing me for work experience at that time. To top it off, he said he would not be working in South Australia either as he was needed at home."

"Was that the end of it? Did he call you or anything?"

"Yes and no. He changed his mobile number, and the landline just went to an answering machine. One early morning, I finally got through and spoke to his mother. She was very blunt, explaining that Tristan would not be contacting me again because I had told him lies about my heritage. She never mentioned the words *colour* or *race* or *Aboriginal*, but I could sense her hostility. I was so shocked that I had difficulty in trying to make her see that I had not lied or tried to deceive Tristan or anything. No secrets. She just said goodbye and hung up. That was that."

"Sarah, I'm so sorry." Elodie spoke softly and moved closer to her friend.

"No, don't be sorry. If that's the type of person he chooses to be, then I'm glad he's gone. I've learned a lesson from all this and have avoided serious relationships since then. The thing that annoys me most is that I had never had any reason to think of myself as being different from anyone else. Now I find I am always defensive when it comes to my family or matters that relate to Indigenous people. I guess he's always been the same and has no intention of changing, but he has altered my view of the world. That's for sure."

Elodie and Ben put their arms around Sarah and hugged her tight. It wasn't long before Elodie's sense of humour got the better of her and she started to giggle.

"I wish I could have seen the look on his face when you introduced him to your parents."

The Bag Lady

My name is Jenny. I was a sometime friend of Alinga.

I found her that day with her arms wrapped firmly around a slender eucalypt, her eyes screwed shut and her dark cheek pressed tightly against the smooth, white bark. Beside her lay the old pram she used to collect handbags and duffels from the bins and op shops around town. Its front axle had broken with the weight, and the wheels now splayed outwards, dipping the pram forward into the gutter and spilling its contents amongst the decaying leaves and accumulated take-away wrappers.

A group of young people across the road at the bus shelter spat on the pavement and mocked her actions, clinging to the timetable pole and moaning loudly about their lost luggage. Other commuters sat passively, mumbling quietly to each other about the state of the world and the social problems of today's youth. Nobody crossed the road to help, preferring not to see her distress and relieved when the bus pulled in, its dusty bulk shielding them from a difficult problem, removing them from the cause of their guilt.

I tried to console her, asking if she wanted me to help somehow. There was no way I could touch the pile of bags and their smelly contents; however, I offered to go around to Vinnies and find another pram. She gave no physical response, but as I left, I heard her whisper a thank-you. I did wonder whether her gratitude was because of my offer or because I was leaving her alone, and I silently admonished her for putting me in this situation.

Vinnies lay just south of the bus and train station in a quiet street off the main shopping strip. They knew her there. Everybody knew the bag lady. I explained the situation and asked for a replacement pram, hoping it would be donated, but no such luck.

"This is supposed to be a charity, for Christ's sake. Surely, you can give that poor woman something for nothing." My anger was evident, and I regretted even getting involved.

"She can pay, you know." The manager appeared from behind stacked boxes of donated goods that would probably end up as landfill by day's end.

"She can pay," he repeated. "She was left the property when her foster parents died. They took her in, looked after her all those years, and see how she turned out. It's a shame. It was the new property that they bought after she left the farm, and the old feller left it to her at his wife's request. Trouble is, because she never actually lived in the new house, she just won't accept it as hers. Her mind is back in the dreamtime, and she prefers to live on the streets. Going walkabout."

He took my money and shuffled back behind his boxes, inhabiting a world he had built for himself amongst other people's discarded paraphernalia. "Not unlike the bag lady," I thought out loud.

"Her name is Alice," he called as I used the pram to push through the finger-marked doors and headed back towards the station.

Alice had released the tree just as the breeze came up from the northwest, promising rain that would settle the dust and wash away footpath grime left by uncaring travellers. I left her that afternoon with the new pram after hauling the old mangled wreck across to an industrial skip that vomited its contents into the rising wind.

She had clung to that tree just as she had clung to her foster mother as a child, holding tight with her face tucked in so the old woman's manicured hands had no room to swing a punch and they fell less heavily on her back and shoulders. That way she avoided the black eyes and bruised legs that were visible to others at school, the marks that required a lie to protect her benefactor. Nobody would have believed the truth anyway, so she chose to be punished for silence, letting them believe she had fallen off her bed, the balcony, the stairs, or the rockery. That afternoon, she had held the tree tight to avoid the verbal punches from irritable youths who waited for the city trains to bring in their weekly stash.

Not many knew her name. She was always referred to as the bag lady, the one who had somehow slipped through the welfare system and only occasionally returned to her room at the hostel. We had spoken over the years, when her words were lucid and her thoughts not yet so stewed. Sometimes on the crowded train where she rocked back and forth with the rhythm of the wheels, sometimes at the bus shelter where she rested and reorganized the bag straps that crisscrossed her chest and shoulders. Before she had the pram and the drivers refused to allow her a seat unless she discarded the baggage, before the lack of symmetry in the concrete paths confused her and she retreated to shrubby creeks and parklands that had hidden her in childhood.

Even back then, she spoke of those who were out to get her, although I never understood who *they* were. She tried to warn us, her words reflecting the years of forced Bible study that *they were out there,* that *they* would take over in the end and there would be none of her people left, nowhere for her to go. She shrugged her laden shoulders and admitted she had nowhere anyway, not since she had been given to the family and was expected to do them proud, show the world what good people they were. There was such intensity in her quietly spoken words that I was obliged to listen, although I did so reluctantly.

Eventually, she stopped using the trains or buses to return to her hostel in the neighbouring town and began sleeping amongst the bundles of clothes dumped thoughtlessly at the charity bins. Occasionally, Vinnies volunteers would put her in the collection truck and drive her home on their way to the municipal tip, but she would be back the next morning, having walked the few kilometres, pushing her pram and reasoning with ghosts that inhabited her past.

If the weather was good, she enjoyed that walk up alongside the highway, feeling the earth spirits lift her feet and connecting her to country that had been worked by her father. If she went in the early morning, before commuters destined for city offices filled the air with the acrid smell of car exhausts and oily bitumen, she could breathe in the earthen scents of freshly ploughed paddocks and dried grasses. She could hear the skylarks spiralling into the warmth of a pale sunrise and marvel at the plovers that noisily guarded their territory day and night. She remembered her name was Alinga, the sun.

Our talks became few and far between the more she deteriorated, and I often crossed the road in order to avoid confrontation. There had been a time when I considered helping her look for the family she remembered from before the accident took her parents and baby brother. But the task was just too hard. What with the lack of community interest, the incessant red tape, the Freedom of Information forms, and her inability to focus or sign, I put the idea aside. After all, she was not my problem.

"They came to find me, you know," she told me in one of her clearer moments, "but the old woman shooed them away, said I wanted nothing to do with them. When they kept coming back, she locked me in my room, said they were rubbish and that she could give me a better home. The old man did nothing, but he never hurt me either. We had a kind of silent understanding.

"I had to call her Mother. I had to go to church and do my homework and keep my hair tidy. I had to wash the dishes and polish the floors and tell people how happy I was, so Mother could hold her head high." Her voice trembled, but no tears came.

There had been a problem with the adoption. New laws that the child did not understand, did not ask about, knowing that they made Mother angry. Only her own kind would be allowed to adopt, and she waited for them to arrive, locked in her room for her own good.

"She's from the Wurundjeri tribe," Mother would tell curious visitors, feigning a knowledge of ancient cultures. "Her mother worked for me in the house while her father helped on the land. She shows no interest in her heritage, fully assimilated, and you can understand why. Her relatives have no time for her, and she's much better off here with us."

Eventually, the child could no longer cope with the unrelenting vigilance and began to retreat from schoolwork and the religious life that had pleased Mother. Her housekeeping ceased to satisfy the old lady, and her meals became less frequent as she strayed farther from home. Before she was out of her teens, the foster parents had sold the house where she still saw her mother's shadows and had moved out of town. There was no discussion, no goodbye, nothing left to fill the suitcase her guardians had given her as an afterthought. Only a removal van that took all her memories, good and bad, and a street of closed doors and hurriedly drawn curtains.

Salvos helped her sign up for welfare, gave her a hostel room down the track for a while. Still, she could not quell the urge to return to the only home she could remember, taking the train daily until obsession filled her perplexed mind with lines she could not cross and steps that stalled her progress. The orderliness that had been forced on her as a child was now her undoing, just as her lack of possessions dictated this urgent collecting of bags.

The room was eventually given to a needier person, they said. One who appreciated the efforts of welfare groups and upheld their charitable presence. It was not really my business, but I had to go and see them.

"What is it with you people?" I argued, angry that they could sit there with their hot tea and fancy cakes. Angry that I should even be involved.

"I checked out your mission statements and believed what they said about you caring for people of other races. When did she fail your criteria for someone needing help? When did she get relegated to the too hard basket?"

Their answer funnily enough did not surprise me. "She doesn't want our help and has chosen to live that way. She's welcome to come and see us, but she has her own money, you know. And a house across town. We can't do anything unless she asks." They had tried but could not change the edicts of her ancestry, they said.

I did not have the patience or the will to reason with them about their supposed principles of helping the needy. I guess there are incompetent individuals within any organization, but I still could not understand how Alice could be left to wander, collecting her payments on Thursdays, sleeping wherever, and only God knows what she did for meals. She did not like to be a bother and did as she was told without argument.

It wasn't so long ago that she stood beside me at the bus shelter, gripping my arm so I could not escape, her wild, wide eyes keeping my attention focused.

She told me about the church that Mother had taken her to as a child and how the stories of good against evil frightened her. Her conversations were always hard to follow, and it was a while before I realized her mind had retreated to the dreamtime stories passed down from her parents and the aunties and uncles she had barely known. Listening to her ramblings about how the land was formed by mythical creatures that eventually became the rocks and rivers, plains and valleys of the world we know, I failed to notice the pallor in her cheeks and the trembling that coursed through her limbs.

It was not until she released her hold and sat down heavily on the cold wrought iron seat that I saw she had another problem. Someone called an ambulance as the bus pulled away, leaving us alone with the dust and debris wind-lifted from pockmarked pavers.

Undernourished, they told me later, with a heart problem to boot. She needed to be institutionalized for her own sake, they said, and she remembered the locked room. A suitable home would be found eventually, they said, releasing her back onto the streets. And the papers lay at the bottom of the pile for more long months while she continued to gather her bags, filling them with scraps that had no meaning.

I watched her that tree day through the bus window, her layered skirts snatched by the wind and tangling in the wheels of the new pram, slowing her anxious progress through the endless crisscrossed lines in the pavement. The youths had returned for their evening session, cadging cigarettes and an occasional dollar from travellers who should have known better. She hurried from them as best she could, the pram wheels turning always in the wrong direction, the senseless taunts pushing her along towards a dusty path worn by years of shuffling schoolchildren.

I knew she often took that creek track to avoid the torment, and on one guilt-ridden occasion, I had followed her, hoping that at the other end there would be a suitable refuge. I doubt that she knew I was there, and I heard her talking to herself, remembering the words used by her father as he told the stories of the old times. The sounds and descriptions rolled easily off her tongue, the lilting rhythm of the words soothing in their repetition, and she spoke them aloud in defiance of Mother's orders.

There was no refuge, only the soft green verge that dipped downwards to the creek and upwards to the trees at the edge of a fenced-off playground. To a place where Alice had often hidden from the jeering and catcalls and prayed the rain would come. They would go home then, leaving her alone to cope with the disorder that now controlled her mind.

That day was the last time I saw her. I imagined how she lay there in the velvet grass and let her tired body absorb the chill night air. Schoolchildren found her in the morning, her dark skin purpled from the frost and icelets at the corners of her eyes. There were no suspicious circumstances, the report said. Her heart had finally given out.

Still they ask questions I cannot answer. After all, she was not my problem. We might have shared the same skin colour, the same dark eyes and wiry hair, but we were not the same.

I never knew the stories.

Kyle

I first met Kyle five or six years ago. At that time, I had been asked to write a series of articles about the people in our community for the local rag where I worked. After lining up several interviews with the usual celebrities, I felt that we needed someone new and a little bit different from those folk our readers were already familiar with, from sports meetings or school and council agendas.

A friend from the Organics Café in town suggested I talk with Kyle. He was a comparative newcomer to this area, young and ambitious with a highflying job in a progressive advertising agency. He was a working resident, a clean-cut and outgoing member of the community. Although he commuted regularly between Melbourne and Sydney, he still fitted the criteria needed for the articles, or so I thought.

Kyle had lived here for about eighteen months, was well liked by his associates and friends, and had recently bought a house on the hillside below the now defunct university. The *posh* part of town he said, where American-style two- and three-storey homes were built over the entire house block, leaving no room for children to play, or for dogs to run. Silver birch and golden rocket cypress filled small grassy pockets that sufficed for front lawns where naked concrete ladies held large bowls aloft to catch dribbling fountains of rusty water. Suburbia in a country town.

We met several times over the next few weeks, sometimes at the café but more often over a hasty lunch at the busy shopping mall. Between his hectic schedule and my other interviews, I discovered a life that held secrets I had heard many times before in whispered conversations and private corners. I had a feeling that this was not the kind of article that would be accepted by my editor, but this young man, who was just discovering his own vulnerabilities and learning to hold his head high despite past criticism, fascinated me. Kyle had grown out of his childhood insecurities and now needed to make a difference in this world of deep-seated prejudices and racial bullying.

Telling his story was one way he could make that difference, yet he still held back, in part, avoiding the truth that would only surface some years later in an environment far removed from this small town where attitudes were ingrown. I continued with the interviews rather guiltily, knowing that his words might not reach his intended audience.

Born on the Gold Coast, Kyle moved with his family to wherever his parents were transferred. Both of his parents worked for the federal police during those early years and happily filled vacancies across the eastern and southern states. As their three children grew and Kyle reached school age, it was decided that the family had to establish roots. Tasmania, with its casual lifestyle and inexpensive housing opportunities, had seemed to be the ideal place to settle and raise the family.

"And it was. It was a great place to live, and I will always think of Tassie as my home, as country." Kyle pulled a serviette from the stack on the food court bench and wiped a smudge that only he would notice, from his burgundy leather dress shoes. In his business clothes he looked a little overdressed for this town, but Kyle was able to pull off the effect he had on others with a casualness learned from necessity.

"But I couldn't stay there," he continued. "Apart from the lack of career opportunities, there were too many encumbrances in my life that held some unpleasant memories."

"Encumbrances?" I questioned him, thinking that this was all about the burden of having an Indigenous father and a white mother. "Surely in this age of growing multiculturalism, there are few problems that laid-back Tasmanians can't cope with?"

"Oh, for sure, although I wouldn't describe Tasmanian people as laid-back. *Old-fashioned*, even *backward*, would be more appropriate." Kyle laughed, aware of his own bluntness, before leaning closer, his chin resting on scrubbed and manicured hands. "There are other things," he said. "I'm Indigenous, I'm atypical, and I'm a heavy-metal fan to top it off." He retreated slightly to better observe my reaction. "And here on the mainland, I am berated for being Tasmanian! Can't win."

I leaned back in my cold plastic chair, just a little surprised by his admission.

"Oh, double whammy! I see why you wanted to move to the mainland. How does all that go down with your family?" My exclamation pleased him for some reason, and I could see, rather than hear, a throaty chuckle that showed in his dark eyes and wide grin.

"I know mainlanders joke about Tasmanians having two heads, and I can't say I'm a fan of heavy metal." I laughed. "But being Indigenous and *camp*? Now that is serious stuff."

Kyle sipped his coffee hot while I waited for mine to cool, savouring the spicy aroma of my first cup for the day and mentally arranging questions that would encourage him to talk. However, it was Kyle who kept the conversation going, and I realized that he had a need to put his life into words, as much for his own benefit as for others.

"I went to school in Somerset, a little town in Tasmania's north. Pretty, isolated, and very insular. I didn't really understand at the time, but the people there still lived in the olden days, believing that there were no original inhabitants anymore. I was taught in school that they'd been wiped out during early settlement and Truganinni was the last of them. You've probably been there yourself, I mean, in the school situation, where history is not questioned. Of course, we now know that there are different versions of history, and we shouldn't believe everything we read."

Kyle also believed those stories at the time, knowing that his own family was from southern Queensland and his dad before that came from Derby in Western Australia. However, he found it very confusing as many of his friends described themselves as First Tasmanians and they told stories of ancestors who had shared their land with whalers and farmers, with convicts and free settlers from the old country. And these stories had been passed down through the generations of Indigenous Tasmanians.

I commented that the 1970s had brought about change in that regard, but Kyle just shook his head and said, "They forgot to tell the Tassy folk then, because we were still being taught that rubbish when I first went to primary school."

We were always teased in school, and my little brothers had an especially hard time because they were darker than me. It was even harder for us than for the other Indigenous kids, because our mum was white. One day, my little brother Elijah came home from school visibly upset but not wanting to tell Mum why. So I persuaded him to tell me and promised that I would keep it to myself. Mum was pretty protective in those days and understood that we were having a difficult time. We didn't tell her much though, because we knew she would march straight down to the school and have a go at anyone who caused trouble. We learnt how to keep secrets." Kyle ordered a second coffee and a vegetarian quiche before continuing.

"Elijah told me that this other kid at school, I remember his name was Jarrod Kronk, had been giving him a hard time because of his colour. Jarrod said that our mum was not our real mother because she was white. He said our dad pooped us out, and that was why we were all shitty brown." Kyle wiped a hand across his brow and shook his head. He never showed any anger, but I could see the hurt in his eyes. "In all my years at school, I never hit anyone for what they called us, but I certainly had no respect for kids who thought like that. My mum always told us that it came from the parents and those kids did not know any better. We learnt to live with the bullying and kept out of trouble as best we could."

At least Kyle was upfront with his lifestyle and ancestry, unlike some other long-term residents here who had tried too hard to fit in with the conservatism of this village and its business people. I recalled Tayo whose deceit had been his ultimate undoing. Tayo could have stayed, but the accident and its aftermath shook him up, releasing the feelings of guilt and shame that he had experienced as a child. He eventually left town, opening a car yard with his cousin in Mildura and slipping easily into the culture of his Latje Latje relatives.

Despite Kyle's openness and work reputation that earned him respect in some corners, I began to doubt that he would fit the profile required for the articles that I had been asked to write. Perhaps he was a little too willing to mess with opinions and too naïve to realize that these people had entrenched ideas about race, religion, and life choices that influenced their acceptance of newcomers. This wasn't his town and never would be.

Leaving his parents and younger brothers behind in Tassie had not been straightforward for Kyle, but he knew what he wanted out of life, and that could not be achieved on the island. Moving to regional Victoria rather than directly into city life made the transition easier, although he quickly learned how to adapt and be accepted within the business and arts centres of Melbourne. An ability to talk his way through job interviews soon landed him a promising career in advertising, and within a year, he had jumped the queues and was winging his way to Sydney every other week. Still, he tried to make a life on the city outskirts where travel to the airport was easy and where he thought he could enjoy the quiet during his days off.

Not so, it seemed, for he had to contend with neighbours who were old school and bitter, resenting the intrusion of this young bachelor who painted his front door purple, grew rustic Aboriginal sculptures in his front yard instead of plants, and had his boyfriend stay over. Kyle took it all in his stride for a while, for he had grown up with the kinds of snide remarks that were now spoken loudly by walkers who passed his gate or residents behind the fence. He would cope, just as he had in Tasmania, by being cheery and polite to those who could not see beyond their own insulated upbringing. After all, most of his time was spent with work colleagues who cared little for old-fashioned protocol and had no time for past prejudices. His neighbours' problems were their own, and he chose to avoid confrontation.

When I approached the editor with my suggestions and the finished story about Kyle, she ticked off the "good" citizens who had appeared in the paper on other issues and barely glanced at the few I had written on newer, less familiar residents. I tried to convince her that people like Kyle were an important part of our future and represented the rampaging growth spurt that this town was experiencing. But no, she wanted staid conservatism, and those she called *queer blacks* were just too different. How could the stability of this town be retained if we publicized newcomers who did not hesitate to break the rules? How could we keep the country atmosphere if we brought in these offbeat young folk who wanted change and cared little for our way of life?

I was offended by her remarks and by her inability to listen. I had difficulty in understanding her reasons for leaving out the ordinary and the perhaps not-so-ordinary people.

"These shorts are to be promotional, commissioned by several of the business people around here. The people you interview must be representational of the way this town should appear to investors and others, like real estate agents, medical staff, and shopkeepers of high standing. Kyle is a fly-by-nighter and won't last the distance. He doesn't represent the solidarity and security that some of our long-term business people have earned over the last decades." The phone rang and she cut me short, indicating that her decision was final.

Kyle too was disappointed, although I had warned him that this might happen. We lost touch for a while after that, and it was a year or so before I decided to call on him again, thinking perhaps I could reintroduce the story to my new editor. I needed to update a few things, but I was also keen to catch up on our brief friendship and perhaps renew the pleasant chats we had had down at the café.

When I pulled into the drive, I noticed the purple door had been graffitied and the welded statues were gone. Weeds protruded through the sandstone pavers, and the barrel mailbox was spilling its junk mail onto the footpath.

An elderly neighbour had seen me get out of the car. I asked him about the house and whether Kyle still lived there, even though it seemed obvious that he had moved on.

"Sold up and went back to country where he belonged, I heard. Renters are in here now, and I wish the heck they'd leave as well. That young fella with his *fancy boyfriend* was at least clean and pretty quiet compared to this lot. I heard they split up because of his job, you know, being away all the time. Don't know where he is now, but I think he should have taken more time to get to know us.

Sure, we heckled him heaps, but he didn't hang around long enough to get to really understand us and find out that we aren't all rotten. Just takes us time to get used to newcomers." The old man smiled then, showing blue gums and yellowed teeth. He had not earned my respect with his half-bitten apology.

I doubted that he would ever have accepted Kyle and his sometime housemate, but often it takes a bad experience to make people see that what they had before was not so difficult to swallow after all.

A few summers later, while on holiday in West Australia, I was shopping at Myers in the busy city centre of Perth, trying to attract the attention of a member of the sales staff. Crowds of shoppers, escaping the intense heat outside, milled around the outlets of Pilgrim and Country Road, Diesel and Industrie, trying on expensive clothing and accessories before heading to the bargain basement or back home to buy at a cheaper rate online. Tired of waiting for service, I put my fingers in my mouth and whistled, not too loudly, to attract the attention of a young man with coloured plates set inside dangling earlobes. He turned, as did all the would-be shoppers, and then headed my way.

It wasn't until he was right beside me that I recognized his easy smile and welcoming handshake.

"Kyle. What a surprise. You're a long way from home. Have you changed careers? Are you working here now?" The questions were spontaneous, and I would have kept going if he hadn't stopped me, indicating a potential buyer, with an armful of expensive garments, in need of attention.

"It's a long story and my boss is watching." Kyle took me by the elbow and guided me away from the crowded spaces between jam-packed clothes racks. "So good to see you again after how many years? How about joining me for lunch? Breaves Café in the mall at twelve, and we can catch up on a bit of gossip. I have so much to talk about. Things have changed, I can tell you."

I was surprised by his enthusiasm and felt the years between our last meeting slip away. Kyle looked different, more offbeat if that was possible, yet he had not aged despite almost reaching that transitional stage of thirty. I felt rather lacklustre in plain jeans and white tee, with crinkles around my eyes and just a hint of grey showing through rather unruly curls. Kyle had darkened in the western sun and had shaved a narrow strip around his head, tying the long top strands into a tight, black ponytail with the rest cut short around his ears. He wore a floral-patterned shirt, with the sleeves rolled high enough to show the effects of regular workouts, dark braces, and skinny, tan jeans. The burgundy shoes were still there but made of canvas instead of patent leather and tied with brash spotted laces. He flashed a chunky silver band on his left hand as he moved to attend his customers and called back to me over the heads of impatient shoppers, "Oh, by the way, I'm engaged!" Someone in the melee clapped and cheered, setting off a brief chain reaction throughout the throng.

It was already late morning, so I decided to find Breaves and sit there with a cool drink while I waited for the lunch rush to begin. I always carry my notebook (the paper kind) and a smooth writing pen to jot down anything I find interesting wherever I travel, so an opportunity to relax and write in the semi-darkened café was welcome. I wanted to ask Kyle about the boomerang he had mentioned during our earlier meetings and why he had moved so far from Tasmania. I had always felt there had been something missing in our interviews, something that Kyle had difficulty in articulating or simply preferred to keep hidden.

He arrived right on time, sauntering into the café where he was obviously well-known and waving to let me know he had seen me tucked away in a far corner. Staff welcomed him with cheek kisses or high fives while one young man gave him a warm and welcoming hug. Kyle took his hand and led him across to my table. Resting his hands on my shoulders, Kyle was eager to introduce me to his friend.

"Chris, I'd like you to meet Linton, my *fiancé*. Linton, this is Chris, my journalist friend from home that I told you about." Kyle grinned broadly as Linton shook my hand. "We're waiting for the West Australian laws to change so we can set a wedding date." It seemed that the years had not changed Kyle as he slid straight into the conversation with no small talk needed to fill the first awkward moments. Linton excused himself, saying he would be back with the menu and ice water.

I needed some explanations. It was difficult for me to understand how this young, ambitious advertising agent had given up a powerful and exciting career to work as a sales manager. However, it did seem to suit his extrovert personality and certainly offered the opportunity to accessorize his flamboyant wardrobe, dressing up to sell fashions. I suppose that, in a way, he was still in the advertising business but was now using himself as a forum rather than catering to the computerized needs of money-hungry and opinionated graphic-marketing executives.

That was my interpretation, but Kyle's comment was far more simple and an insight into the traumas of his childhood.

"You see, I managed the teasing and trickeries of my school years by ignoring the bullies and telling my brothers to do the same. It wasn't as bad as in my dad's day when some of the parents got together demanding that the Indigenous kids have a special school of their own. They said they were doing it for the good of those kids, but in reality, they were afraid that some of the black dirt would rub off on their own children. When I went to secondary college, I no longer had to worry about Elijah and Ben, so I just handled the name-calling by avoiding trouble and by pretending that my enemies were really my friends. Eventually, they just gave up. They always did. Now I look back and I think about how hard I tried to fit in, be the best in class, in sport and in friendships.

"I worked equally as hard when I left school, but one day, one of the guys at work saw how exhausted I was after a particularly heavy few months and said to me, 'Slow down. You don't have to prove yourself, Kyle, or convince everybody that you are as good as them. Don't try so hard. You *are* as good as the rest of us, if not better. So relax and enjoy the journey.' He shocked me a bit because I had not realized that that was what I had been doing all those years. Trying to prove myself, trying to show the bullies that they were wrong. That just because I was Aboriginal did not mean that I was, you know …" He frowned as he searched for an appropriate word. "Inadequate."

Linton was waiting for us to order. Kyle stuck to his usual vegetarian diet and suggested I have the same. Within minutes, Linton brought out crisp bruschetta slices piled with semi-dried tomatoes and feta cheese, served on mismatched plates in earthy, desert colours. He apologized for not being able to sit and chat for a while, squeezed Kyle's shoulder lightly, and disappeared behind the kitchen screen. I would have liked to hear his version of their meeting and how he dealt with the inevitable taunts that would come their way.

Kyle rearranged the food on his plate and continued the conversation.

"It was a real wake-up call, and I started to question what I really wanted in life. Telling you the stories from my childhood also helped change the way I thought, and I began to look deeper into my heritage. Mum and Dad had always told us not to be ashamed, but they didn't realize, by just saying that, they made me wonder what there was to be ashamed about. I mean, why would somebody mention shame if there was no reason? That got me thinking. They also taught us to be proud of our ancestors, and I was, of course. But it is only recently that I have developed an avid curiosity about my dad's people, and I just want to learn more. I am intensely proud of my Indigenous background. But there is shame too, and one small, fairly insignificant incident that happened when I first arrived here in Perth still makes me cringe with embarrassment."

The hour had gone so quickly, and Kyle had to get back to work. He left me more curious than ever about his recent past, but I would have to wait a few days to speak with him again. It seemed entirely appropriate that this young man had moved into the retail sector, peddling fancy clothes from Italy and France, showing customers labels that promoted stylish garments as "Australian designed and owned" and sidestepping the smaller "Made in China" signs. He was not being dishonest, just doing what he had always done, avoiding truths that would not change attitudes anyway. It was difficult for Kyle to throw off the old nuances from his school days, but I could see that he was becoming increasingly aware of his own ability to change the way people viewed his lifestyle choices and his Indigenous inheritance.

The weekend came and went without a call from Kyle. I needed to return to my own hometown and despaired that he had forgotten his promise to tell me some stories about his dad's childhood. By Tuesday, after I had left a dozen messages on his phone, Kyle finally answered.

"I went *walkabout.*" He laughed over the phone. "Living up to my reputation. No, seriously, Linton and I took a few days off work so I could introduce him to my extended family in Broome. Had a great time, but I have to admit I did forget that you needed to catch a flight home soon. Sorry about that. Just to make up, I have brought back some old photos for you to look at and a few new ones for you to keep. Meet us down by the Swan River this arvo? Riverside Café, and I'll shout you a lunch."

It was a beautiful day with a gentle breeze, so lunch by the river sounded good to me, especially as someone else was paying. Restaurants along the river are not cheap, but they do have a reputation for fresh food and relaxing views. A tourist's paradise.

Kyle and Linton lived not too far from the river, in an East Perth unit overlooking the Wellington Street Park, where the evening congregations of Aboriginals annoyed some white residents. To Kyle they were friends greeting him cheerily as he made his way home from work and making small talk about the weather, the government, or family squabbles. Despite his paler skin, and some misunderstandings along the way, they recognized him as a brother, and he happily acknowledged that relationship.

Barramundi steak with a lightly seasoned mango and avocado salad slowed our conversation for a while, but Kyle was soon his old self, relating incidents from his past that affected his acceptance of whatever the future would bring.

"Dad was born under a tree, you know. I'm not joking. In Broome, I met with my paternal grandmother. We called her Ninni, but I am not sure of the origins of that name. I get so frustrated because I still have so much to learn about my family history and the old people are fast disappearing. Ninni is a little, frail, old lady now, and no one really knows when she was born. She told me that when the Japanese invaded Broome back in 1942 or thereabouts, all the women and children were evacuated inland. That's where my father was born, under a tree in desert country. Not many Australians can say they entered this world in such an exotic location and manner."

Kyle looked pleased with that knowledge and was obviously proud to share the things he had learned from his grandmother. He showed me some of the photos of her as a young woman but said he was not allowed to take any of her now that she was nearing her final days.

She was and still is a strong-minded woman. Her husband had signed up to protect this country and went off to war. He never came back, and it is only in the last few years that his contribution has been acknowledged. That's the way it was, I guess. Anyway, Ninni moved north to Derby, raising her two boys by herself, making sure they were educated properly in the white man's way. It was at home that she taught them the old stories and the meanings of life that she had learned from her parents. Ninni somehow balanced her culture with a deep loyalty to the church, and she still believes in a Christian God.

Kyle's parents had split up before he moved to Western Australia. His father returned to Derby on the west coast, where the salty ocean winds dumped sand into backyards and open car windows. Where the feeling of isolation spurned travellers and would-be residents. For those who stayed the isolation brought a sense of comfort and encouraged loyalty within family or work groups. Kyle's Dad had missed that instinctive bonding and eventually travelled back to the fishing village to reclaim his roots.

It was his return that enabled and encouraged Kyle to explore his ancestral histories and learn more about the family that he so eagerly acknowledged as his own. Now there was a sense of urgency as the old ways disappeared along with those who could remember. This was another reason for Kyle to leave his hectic life in advertising and take on the less rigid timetable of retail manager. He needed time to learn the stories before they were no more, and Perth was the ideal base from which to gain that knowledge.

With lunch over, we said goodbye to Linton and headed back to the store. Kyle told me about his father and how, as an important elder, he is the keeper of some treasured artefacts. Stepping up the pace, Kyle jokingly put his hands together and looked to the heavens in mock prayer.

"Please, Dad, if there is one thing I really want to inherit when you are gone, it's the boomerang. The big one with all the worn-out pockmarks."

"What is that supposed to mean?" I questioned Kyle on this sudden outburst.

"People used to think that the Aboriginal communities scorned possessions as they lived a nomadic life, especially the desert tribes. In reality though, they carried with them their hunting gear and food-gathering stuff. But they also had special boomerangs that were not used as weapons or tools. They were ceremonial boomerangs and were handed down through the generations. Dad has one that he would let us touch when we were kids, passed down from his grandfather. We used to run our fingers over the time-smoothed wood and imagine barefoot dancers with dust swirling around their painted bodies. Decorations were daubed on the wood for each special occasion and then rubbed off afterwards. That's the only thing I really want, but before it becomes mine, I have to learn more about its use and its history. I doubt that I will ever know the whole story, but I'll be grateful to just have some kind of knowledge. Maybe I will learn to dance as well."

Kyle did an impromptu stomp on the footpath, much to the delight of some small, dark-eyed children who cheekily imitated this smooth-skinned stranger with the stretched ear lobes.

"But wait. There's more," he said as he laughed at his own parody on that infamous TV ad. "I have kept a little secret from you, if you remember. Something that makes me just a bit ashamed. Insignificantly minor to anyone else, but something that remains at the back of my mind always.

"You see, when I first came to Perth, I was confused and totally in awe of the black people I saw everywhere. I found those circles of Indigenous folk in the park rather confronting. A bit fearsome in my inexperienced mind. Nothing like Tasmania. I was warned to keep away from them, but I soon learned their attitude was inherent, a kind of protection that they had developed over years of racial intolerance. I was actually more threatened by drunks leaving the pubs just as I made my way home from work—white guys full of bitterness and hatred, drinking away the money they earned during the early years of the mining boom when relationships had no chance of surviving the distances. The heat and the loneliness eventually destroyed their families.

"Anyway, as I said, I was a bit wary of them at first and, knowing that whites shunned them, I found myself hiding my own ancestry or at least not flaunting the fact that I had an Aboriginal father. One day, I was shuffling my way along a bus queue, and this old guy came up to me. He was black as sin, with long, grey hair and rheumy eyes that locked with mine before he spoke. 'What mob you from, bro?'"

Kyle tried to ignore him, but he spoke again with a confident, confronting attitude that showed this old blackfella knew his skin colour and wore it proudly. "You know, what tribe your kin come from, up north?"

Kyle said he hesitated before answering quietly, politely so as not to rile the old man. "No, I'm Tasmanian. I come from Tasmania. I'm not from any of your mob."

A burst of raspy laughter from the man made the crowd notice the conversation as Kyle looked away, trying to discourage any further questions.

He looked at me and said in almost a whisper, "I have not told anyone of this and you might think it petty, but I am so ashamed of that denial. There was no real reason for me to say I was Tasmanian, to say I had no family here. That was a turning point for me as I thought long and hard about it afterwards. Anyway, the old fella wasn't going to be put off that easily, and he kept up the questions. 'Nah, you got our blood in yer, boy. No doubt about that all right. I reckon you from Bardi country. What's yer family name?'

"He seemed so sure of himself, so I stood up straight, looked him in the eye, and told him my dad came from the Broome/Derby region, my grandmother was Bardi, and that my mum still lived in Tasmania. I was totally amazed that this guy could recognize not only my Indigenous inheritance, but which part of this enormous land my folk had come from."

For weeks afterwards, Kyle would catch his image in the mirror, party photographs, or shop windows and try to fathom just how anyone could identify his blood rights, especially in such a chance meeting with no prior knowledge. However, that brief and spontaneous denial had caused him shame that he found difficult to shake. It would stay with him for many years.

It was several months after that incident that Linton moved into the East Perth apartment with Kyle. For a while, things were peaceful and fun, but eventually the mobs in the park got wind of this new development and began to change their attitude to Kyle, some hassling him as he got off the bus each evening, others simply avoiding his company.

"You see, I think they felt my relationships and lifestyle had betrayed them somehow. So the heckling started all over again, and I had to put up my mental protection barriers just as I had done back in your town. 'Sister girls,' they called us, although I felt that we did not quite fit that portrayal. We thought of ourselves simply as flatmates going about our business just like any other people. I also felt I had to win back their trust, and gradually, over time, I did just that."

My time was up. I had a plane to catch. It seemed that we had barely scratched the surface of Kyle's life, despite discussing episodes that began with his birth and the difficulties he faced through childhood, into a time when money and prestige mattered. His ability to avoid confrontation and gather friends around him enabled Kyle to succeed, not only in business matters but also in his personal life. Despite the taunts and traumas, Kyle believed his life was good. He was happy with his newfound family and immensely honoured to be a custodian of two cultures.

Back in my old hometown, I felt somewhat let down and disillusioned by the static attitudes of my associates. While I agree times have changed and those living on the margins of accepted behaviour are less ostracized than they were ten years ago, we still have a long way to go before tolerance is the norm. Nonetheless, this remains a small town with inherited prejudices and a home-grown newspaper editor who cannot escape the commercial demands imposed on him by his those who control local establishments.

So much of Kyle's story remains untold. When I first spoke to him, I felt that something was missing, that he held back some kind of secret. I know now that it was his own insecurities he hid beneath a veil of cultivated confidence. It would take many years for him to lose those anxieties and relax in his own skin.

I think about him often and wonder if he has been able to satisfy the insatiable curiosity about his ancestry that drove him to the outback towns of Western Australia.

Digging Up Guman

Dust circulated as the hot, north winds rose over the torn and tormented hills. The developers unloaded more heavy machinery into the cyclone wire cages while yellow-vested workers climbed onto their tractors, the engines breathing fumes into the already polluted morning air.

Bianca stood near the bridge, her sunrise run stalled as she watched the destruction, saw the scarring as though layers of skin were being ripped from the grassy slopes. She was suddenly overcome by unexplained emotion as she felt the gritty air whip across her cheeks. They were digging up her ancestry, the bones of her grandfather, the stories of his birth and survival as the Jackson and Evans settlers moved across these hills, displacing the people who had hunted and danced across the rocky knolls for eons.

She was not against progress and loved the way her town had embraced the city-style living with new shopping centres, cinemas, and any number of entertainment venues. But this was an intrusion she had not anticipated, a darkness descending on her light, bright, suburban existence.

Bianca struggled against her feelings on the way back to her apartment. She blamed the sudden onset of sentiment on her recent divorce, going over and over her feelings about selling the house and moving to the unit. Memories that had been embedded in her acquired furniture and things, stuff, paraphernalia now gone, disposed of in garage sales and at Cash Converters. Leftover memories thrown into the wheelie bin with vases, Tupperware, excess cutlery, and old magazines.

They had been good memories for the most part, but now Bianca needed to be alone with new things that did not send her mind spiralling back to those past few months together when sharing had not been fun. The old things touched by that other woman while Bianca was at work held no pleasure for her anymore.

She sought an explanation for her new feelings and deep down knew that they had no basis in her husband's infidelity or in the sudden separation. She actually enjoyed her new, independent life.

This emotion was different and probably went farther back than she could remember, back to the stories her mother and grandmother had told her, about how these hills had provided shelter for her kin and how the mobs of roos, in their hundreds, bounded down the slopes that were now stripped of life. Bianca had left the country life in her late teens, but something had drawn her back a few years later, something that she felt but could not articulate.

She told herself the unearthing of Guman shouldn't matter. It meant nothing. After all, her grandmother had once admonished her for telling schoolmates that her grandfather was a blackfella. That was private and only for the family to know. To tell others meant trouble and even her teacher had said she should not place such importance on her heritage. Just accept that she was Australian and be glad she had a white-enough skin.

But grandmother and the teacher were from last century, for Christ's sake. Her mother just didn't care one way or the other; in fact, she cared little about anything except the local pokies and a tipple more often than not. And anyway, what did they mean by "a white-enough skin"?

Bianca stomped about the apartment, an anger rising in her head. She questioned this new sensation that threatened to break away from the old, placid, and tolerant person she was content with. "Why now? What has made me so irate?" She spoke aloud, addressing the city views that had so attracted her to this place.

As she watched, the sky blackened and raindrops hit her window. The warmth of the morning and the sudden break in that savage wind could be a precursor to a storm, and she had plans for the day. This fuelled her irritation, although Bianca had never been demonstrative and generally kept any dissatisfaction hidden.

By the time she had showered and was ready to go out, the storm had hit, and even though it was still morning, the lightning was visible across Mount Newitt, tearing the dark sky apart and playing havoc with the now flickering streetlights.

Torrents of heavy raindrops beat against the window as she grabbed her keys and headed for the car. Bianca nosed the VW out of her car space into the storm and stopped. "Too heavy," she muttered as she waited for a break, watching the road rapidly fill with greasy water. Twenty minutes later, she was still there, unsure about whether to go back or venture into the downpour. From her driveway, she could see the development on the hillsides, where terraces had been graded to build apartments and dual living complexes.

Suddenly, Bianca saw the earth move, and she turned her wipers on to see more clearly. The hillside was awash, slipping down towards the already heavily silted creek. The terraces had formed dams, and some of their supporting walls were collapsing, increasing the landslide that threatened to remove the hilltop and fill the little valley.

"Oh, shit. See what you have done." Distraught, Bianca thumped her hands against the steering wheel. "That was my granddad's resting place. God, he was born there, and now you have destroyed everything!" She yelled into the enclosed confines of her car, not really caring if some of her neighbours heard.

It was much later that Bianca realized how important the stories told to her during her childhood had been. They had formed her, given her a history and a tolerance, an attachment to the land where she had grown up. She had never met her grandfather, and the grandmother she knew had been his third wife, taken when he was quite old and she was just a girl. Gran had always told her that when he died his bones were spirited away and buried beneath the trees where he had been born. She never questioned the legalities of those actions when she was a child but had often wondered, as she grew older, how the family had managed to put him back into the land he loved, into the summer hunting grounds of his ancestors.

It was not until the following morning that Bianca could check out the destruction to the new estate, and she found herself pushing through a crowd of excavators, labourers and councillors. The newspaper people were there, along with a dozen curious onlookers and early morning runners. The workers could not enter the site until the mud and broken walls had dried, preventing tractors from going in to begin repairing the storm's damage. That pleased Bianca, as now she had some time to walk to the hilltop and the twisted gum that she had been told was Guman's resting place. By evening, with the day's sun drying the crusted terraces and the workers long gone, she was able to climb around the wire barricades and walk across the precarious channels of heavy clay and on up the hill.

The ancient tree with its wind-whipped and twisted trunk leaned to one side, pushed over by the relentless graders, its roots cut and carved and protruding from the mud, its broken branches bleeding dark sap onto the soggy ground. Bianca, resting on an outcrop of scoria, was startled to find that she was not alone. Down the opposite slope a bit, a dark-haired man searched amongst the graded furrows, stopping every now and then to pick up and examine his finds. Without fear, Bianca called to him, but he did not answer and kept about his business. Curious now, she moved closer to see what he was searching for, her own eyes keeping tight watch on the clumped tussocks and torn earth.

Within minutes, she saw what she had been intent on finding but hesitated to move closer, concerned that she would be revealing her secret to an intruder. Just metres away, a white protrusion was visible in the red gravel, washed clean by the gentler rains that had followed the storm. She stood for a time, glancing from the find to the stranger. At that moment, the man raised his head, and she saw his eyes glance in her direction.

Bianca made a decision. She turned and walked back past the tree and down the slope towards the creek. She would return later when there were no others to see her examine the bones, if that is what they were, and could only hope that the stranger on the hillside did not exhume them in the meantime. Past secrets were still haunting her, and she could not find any legitimate reason to explain her presence to the man. The authorities would certainly intervene if they knew about the burial. There would be questions, and Gran's warning about keeping things private ran circles in her brain. And if they were human bones, how would she take them back with her? What was she supposed to do with a basket of bones that might belong to a roo or a sheep for all she knew? One thing she was sure of was that if the workers came across any remains, they had learned to just cover them with earth and pretend they did not exist. Otherwise, the excavation would be put on hold as do-gooders scoured the land for more artefacts or remains of archaeological importance. Time meant money, and no relics were important enough to stall developers intent on laying concrete slabs as soon as the levelled land had settled.

It was several weeks before Bianca had the time to continue her search, and she was becoming irritated with her own inability to prioritize. While the urgency to find and remove her grandfather's remains hammered in her head, she hesitated and found excuses, convincing herself that nothing mattered, that digging up Guman would change nothing and would only cause more problems in the long run. The summer days were getting shorter, and by the time she arrived home from work, daylight had begun to wane. The longer she put off making a decision, the faster the evening dark crept over her life. Weekends were filled with the usual household or shopping chores or checking on Gran's needs, while visiting friends often stayed longer than she would have liked.

Since her separation, Bianca had learned to appreciate the solitude and often resented intrusion by others. Gran said this feeling must be inherited, handed down from times when family groups were small and the silence of the bush was comforting. She too had found delight in her own company although she had always put the social needs of her children and grandchildren first.

Bianca chose the times for her early morning runs when others were still rising. She avoided built-up areas where the smell of shampoo and soap seeped through bathroom louvres as commuters prepared for work. She resented the smokers who stood shivering on front porches, puffing acrid smoke to mix with exhaust fumes as early drivers inched their cars down excessively steep driveways in the poorly planned hillside estates. A house with a view seemed desirable, but unscrupulous builders, avoiding high excavation and drainage costs, failed to inform buyers of the impracticalities of parking a car on concrete that either rose or fell sharply, depending on which side of the road it was constructed. Great for skateboarders who left their run to school and station until the last minute, shooting carelessly out onto the footpath, heedless of joggers or dog walkers.

She listened to the sound of her runners thumping on the newly constructed concrete walking track, concentrating on landing lightly so as not to disturb the silence of the bush. The path wound alongside the eroded creek banks and through remnant yellow box woodlands, ending abruptly at the bare hillside where heavy machinery lay like dormant leviathans against a backdrop of lightening sky.

Bianca was well and truly home before the skateboarders hit the street and traffic noise from the freeway swelled into the rising light. The dark stranger had not returned as far as she knew, and the workers had not progressed to the higher land where the bones lay. They were too busy repairing storm damage and building access roads on the lower slopes before winter winds brought more rain to slow the digging. English trees had been planted in the recently constructed nature strips, their leafless branches testimony to the harsh conditions and heavy, clay soils. Planting natives would have been more practical, Bianca thought every time she passed that way. In her mind, she imagined the hardy wattles and blackwoods that had once adorned these hills, providing shelter for the roos and bandicoots that sustained her ancestors.

Another weekend passed, and another, before Bianca made up her mind to resume the search. She hesitated telling Gran about her efforts. Unsure about what reaction she would get from the old lady, Bianca decided to wait and see what results the search would bring before broaching the subject of burial and body theft and learning just how the family managed to transport her Guman up the hill. An absence of tracks at that time would have meant a steep climb through tangled grasslands, and they would have needed digging tools as well. She shook her head in private disbelief. A flash of doubt crossed her mind, and for a second, she wondered if maybe she had been duped. Was this another of Gran's dreamtime stories that had filled her childhood? Did the spirit of

Guman really roam these hills, or was it something that she wanted to be true so badly that she believed everything Gran and Mum had told her? The only way for her to uncover the truth would be to find the bones and confront her aging grandmother while she remained lucid enough to understand.

Winters here unfolded slowly, and Bianca still had time to search before chill winds whipped across Mount Newitt, carrying grit from the denuded escarpments, irritating her eyes, and cutting into her skin. This Sunday, when there were no trucks pointlessly ferrying soil and rock from one section just to dump it farther down, she pulled a beanie tightly around her ears, pocketed some gardening gloves, and set off with a trowel in her backpack, intent on finding her grandfather's last resting place.

The tree that she knew as the burial spot had died during the past weeks, littering the ground with grey and brittle leaves that exuded the scent of eucalyptus as Bianca crushed them beneath her sneakers. Her search lasted well into the afternoon, but no bones were found. Nothing. Disillusioned and somewhat disappointed, she headed down towards the creek, now planted with spiked grasses and broadleaved swamp plants set in holes poked through ugly weed mats and netting. She could not help thinking that it looked better the way it was, with the unruly weeds providing habitat for frogs and water rats and a myriad of birdlife.

A car was parked on the service road that ran along the other side of the creek, dwarfed by oversized houses piled like toy building blocks against the backdrop of Mount Newitt's twin. These two hills had filled Bianca's childhood with wonder as Gran packed picnic lunches and the family set off in the early-morning mists for a day of storytelling amongst the red rocks and tiny caves that filled the western slopes.

That's him. That's the dark guy I saw after the storm. What's he doing here? Bianca thought as she walked and watched the car driver load something into his car and drive slowly away. *No wonder I could find no bones. He's probably taken them all.* She felt hurt and angry with herself for not coming sooner. *Probably an archaeologist or something. As long as he is not from the law, or the council or anywhere that might be interested in the origins of the bones. Oh, Gran, what have you got me into?* There was nothing to be done, so Bianca headed home, dejected and just a bit curious about the other searcher.

Several weeks later, wandering around the local craft market with its dwindling number of stallholders, Bianca tripped over a sandbag that weighted the tie ropes of a sombre grey marquee. The owner came from behind his trestle table, apologetic and concerned, either for her welfare or for the trouble he could face if she was hurt. Bianca bit her tongue, controlling the curses that threatened to undermine her peaceful browsing and draw unwanted attention to herself. In an instant, she recognized the stallholder as the same man who had poached the bones from her hill. Angrily, she shook off his helping hand and sat on his chair to nurse a swelling ankle.

"I know you. I saw you on the hill after the rains, pilfering stuff that does not belong to you. Then in the car, just the other day, loading up with something you had probably found and taken without getting permission."

The man laughed after a momentary hesitation. "Bones. I was collecting bones for my sculptures."

"My grandfather's bones," she hissed, "and you have probably chopped them all up to make this." She swept her arms out, indicating the marquee items. It was only then that she saw the artwork. Beautiful items of what seemed like ivory, smoothed and sculpted into elegant, flowing pieces that glowed warmly under a carefully placed solar lantern. Snakes wrapped around tree trunks, beetles atop toadstools with elongated stems, birds perched or flying, and a bowl filled with glowing, pink, quartz marbles. A small statue caught her eye, the figure of an Aboriginal warrior sitting cross-legged on a piece of red scoria the size of her fist. The man was carved in white bone material, spirit like and entrancingly smoothed with features that were left more to the imagination rather than the eye of the viewer. She ran her fingers down the delicate spear he held in one outstretched hand, its base firmly embedded in the rock close to his knee.

"You like that one?" the seller asked. "I collected a special piece of bone on Mount Newitt, beneath that sad twisted gum that the tractors had destroyed. I had no idea what it had come from, but its shape and colour inspired this little carving. It seemed appropriate to seat him on the scoria I sourced directly from the hill. To me, it represents all the lives of original inhabitants who had been lost as settlers moved into the area. This is the spirit of those people."

Bianca repeated her comment that these bones could have been her grandfather's and added angrily that he had no right to presume that he could represent her ancestors in this or any other manner. His answer surprised her, and she felt a little guilty.

"These are my people too, and I think I have every right to portray them in any way that speaks to me." His voice was quiet now, and he spoke slowly, no longer sympathetic to the pain in her ankle. "I doubt that your grandfather was buried on the hilltop. If this is his resting place, then he was probably buried, or left, closer to the camp that would most likely be near a water source—the creek. Or the local church graveyard. Is that what you were looking for the first day I saw you?"

Bianca glanced at him then, surprised that he had recognized her from that day last summer. It was then that she truly noticed his dark skin and pale palms, his heavy brow and thick, wiry curls that reminded her of Gran. It passed her mind that he was handsome in a rugged sort of way, although his Aztec-style poncho did little to enhance those looks.

"I was not pilfering, by the way," he continued. "I had the permission of the landowner, on one condition—that I keep any finds to myself. And he made me put that in writing. I told him what I was looking for and said he could do what he liked with anything else that was hidden there." He laughed. The memory obviously struck a chord with him but left Bianca puzzled.

"There were no human bones, I can assure you. These are all from animals, cows and sheep mostly, with an occasional wild dog, and once I found a snake carcass. That was too fresh, so I left it on the hillside for the landowner to deal with. I prefer to use old bones to make a powder; otherwise, I would simply go to the supermarket and buy soup bones. You see, the ancient, flaky bones grind easily and mix well with the resin. They give me a substance that suits my way of modelling. Some of them I colour, but others, like this spirit man, I prefer to leave white and pure with occasional marbled patches creating authenticity.

Bianca had calmed down and tried to explain. "You don't understand. Guman was buried there, on the hilltop, beneath the trees that used to grow in that area. I know because when he died, my mum and Gran managed somehow to take him away and bury him in the place he said he was born." She sighed and thought how ridiculous this must sound, and why was she bothering to explain to a stranger anyway?

"I saw that the estate threatened to destroy all that side of the hill and decided it was time to retrieve Guman. Put him somewhere else. I don't really know what I expected to find, and I don't know how I was going to carry him away by myself. I am not even sure how I would have felt if I did find human bones there. It's been a long time, since before I was born. Even my mum does not remember him much, and Gran was still quite young when he died. What worried me most was the legality of the whole thing. How would I explain away the bits of skeleton literally hidden in the bottom of my closet?"

Customers fingering the elegant statues pretended not to listen to the conversation, occasionally glancing furtively at Bianca and the artist.

"Ah, might as well introduce myself now that we have shared some rather personal secrets. I'm Jordan, sculptor extraordinaire." He gave a perfunctory bow and grinned broadly at Bianca, expecting her to follow through with her name.

She hesitated, however, and backed towards the marquee entrance, annoyed by his mock vanity. "I'm still angry, you know. Angry at the developers for ruining that land, angry at Gran for not telling me more about my family, and at Mum for just avoiding anything that mattered to me. Mostly I'm angry at you for taking bones that might belong to my family and for presuming that I can just stand here admiring your work while you just grin and pretend it means zilch."

Bianca left without giving her name. Leaving the market and dodging cars on the main road, she walked quickly down a side street through the chilly spring air, silently admonishing herself for being so rude. It also passed her mind that Jordan was really quite attractive, and she shook her head in disbelief that she could even consider thinking of him in that way. The spirit statue kept reappearing in her thoughts, and she had to admit that Jordan's talent was impressive. Bianca slowed and then stopped, thoughtful and agitated. Her ankle was painful, her mind disturbed.

"Really, that statue should be mine. It's probably Guman, his bones mashed into that ridiculous resin." Bianca looked around, suddenly aware and slightly embarrassed that she was thinking aloud. No one heard her on the empty street, doors were closed in the houses, but she still felt rather silly and had an urge to hurry home to the protection of her small apartment.

*****

Gran was feeling the restrictions of her age. She dreaded the oncoming heat of another summer, and her memory had been playing up lately. She often called Bianca to come over and help around the place, a job her daughter should be doing. Bianca's Mum disappeared frequently, hightailing it interstate where she could play the pokies without being recognized. If she had a good win, she would Greyhound it to Mildura or Sydney and somehow return weeks later when times were bad. Internet betting had not yet taken a hold on her and Bianca was thankful, as she preferred it if Gran could not see the self-destruction. Out of sight, out of mind, and the weeks she had alone with her grandmother were more tolerable without having to worry about her mother as well.

As she did the rounds of cleaning the old house where she had spent much of her childhood, Bianca listened to the stories her gran repeated over and over. Always the same, just as they had been told to Mother as a young child, about the dreamtime and how the spirit people had set down laws that must be followed. About why the Galah sported a bald patch and how the hills were formed and where the sacred lands lie. She heard again the meanings of ceremonies and the duties of a good wife or husband. As the old lady's memory faded, she forgot that she had cautioned her young granddaughter about telling people that her ancestors were the first Australians. She spoke of her elderly husband with pride, remembering the gentleness and the way he worked so hard on the land to provide for his growing family. They had little time together, and he was gone before their daughter reached her teens.

"His kidneys were shot," Gran recalled, "so he could work no longer. I got a job and looked after him at home as best I could. But he was an old man, and he got all the blackfella problems. Not the alcohol. He never drank. But his kidneys went anyway, and the diabetes got to him as well. He died in the hospital long before you were born. We cremated him soon after and scattered his ashes up there on the hill where all the twisted gums grew. He's still there now, back with his folks in country he loved."

Bianca dropped the bucket of hot, soapy water she had been carrying to clean the bathroom, spilling its contents over the tiles and watching it seep into the adjoining carpet. Stunned at what Gran had told her, it was several moments before she reacted, grabbing towels and dishcloths to soak up the mess. Gran seemed not to notice, settling back in her recliner with closed eyes and crossed hands.

"Cremated? You had him cremated? You always told me you and Mum had buried his bones on the hillside. Now you tell me he was cremated?" Bianca ferried wet towels to the sink, squeezing out the soapy water before returning to mop some more. She found it hard to believe that so much water could have been contained in one small bucket.

Gran gradually recovered from her dream world of memories and watched Bianca struggling to keep the water from spreading farther across the carpet.

"Of course, we cremated him. There wasn't much left of him when he died. Disease had taken its toll and wasted him away to skin and bones. It was the right thing to do, and anyway, he wanted his ashes returned to the soil where he had been born. Your mum helped me take the urn up the hill, and we had a little ceremony there with the roos looking on and the wedge-tailed eagles soaring higher and higher, just like they were celebrating his freedom. It was a beautiful day. But there are splashes up the wall you've missed. What were you thinking?" Gran had come back to the real world and admonished Bianca for being so clumsy. Mostly, though, she was irritable with her own inability to get out of the chair and help.

"Oh Gran. I wish you had told me earlier. I've been searching for Guman's burial spot ever since the land was sold to that property group. I thought it was his bones you had buried, and there was this guy ... I yelled at him and told him he was pilfering."

Bianca felt her face heat up as she thought back to her rudeness and her presumption that Jordan had stolen her grandfather's bones. She felt stupid and remembered that even she had doubted the story about the burial in the past. In a way though, the revelation was a relief, and she no longer had to fear being caught out with human bones in her possession. Nobody would question the occasional piece of cow's or sheep's leg she had secreted away in her broom cupboard, afraid to put them in her wheelie bin even after she had done the research and identified them as farm animals, not human remains.

****

The following month, the craft market promised to be a washout, but Bianca had decided that she needed to apologize to the sculptor. She loved the rain and knew that the streets would be empty of other walkers if the weather looked foul. Nobody would be exercising their dogs, and only occasionally would she catch a glimpse of other mad joggers, hoodies flapping loose and leggings muddied from the spray off saturated runners. She wondered why people were so afraid of getting wet, preferring to watch through rain-streaked windows in overheated houses, televisions flashing weather reports and news of cars piled up on slippery roads.

A few marquees had been set up in the car park, but most stallholders had moved inside the old gym, their precious crafts and imported goods laid out on dry, velvet-covered trestles. Only a few hardy sellers braved the weather, and Bianca noticed the aged grey canvas of Jordan's stall as soon as she entered the main road. Half-heartedly, she told herself that was good; he had chosen to endure the rain and set up his artwork regardless of whether or not there would be any customers. Another part of her had been hoping that he would not turn up for the day as she was going to find apologizing rather difficult.

There was something else. The little statue had attracted her, and she decided it should be hers, even though she now knew the truth about her grandfather and his ashes. Bianca was never one for knick-knacks around the home, but something about the statue had been on her mind for the past few weeks. Or was it the sculptor? After all, he was handsome, industrious, and independent, and they had a common ancestry as well.

"Careful, girl," she whispered to herself. "Don't expect too much, or you will be disappointed again."

Jordan stood at the entrance to the marquee, checking the grey sky and adjusting the tent flaps to protect his craftwork. He did not notice Bianca as she came closer and he stepped backwards into her path, knocking her down into the muddied gravel.

"Not again!" he exclaimed as he helped her to her feet. "We have to stop meeting like this."

"That's a bit lame. You could at least have said sorry or come up with something newer. I might have broken my ankle this time, and all you can offer is some old cliché that is well past its use-by date. Can you do something about the mud all over my clothes instead of just standing there looking pathetic?"

"OK. OK. No need to yell at me. It was an accident, and I am sorry if you are hurt. Maybe you should watch where you are going."

"Oh, now you are putting the blame on me, and all I did was come here to buy your silly statue. If you still have it, that is. But I am not sure I want it now. If this is the way you treat your customers, you won't be making any sales today." Bianca took the towel he offered and rubbed the mud from her leggings. Then she deliberately cleaned her sneakers, leaving greasy black marks lumped across the white cloth before shoving it back into his hands.

Jordon ignored her outburst. "Which statue were you after?"

"The warrior on the rock. It is not here, so I guess you have sold it already. Not important. I'm off now." Bianca indicated the marquee door but stayed where she was, dripping onto the canvas floor mat. Jordan was rummaging around beneath the trestle table, apparently with no interest in whether she went or not. He came up with a small, square, wooden box hand-painted with dots and lines in the yellows, browns, and reds of the arid outback.

"Before you leave, this is for you. It kinda makes up for all the misunderstandings along the way. Sorry about the accidents, and sorry for the confusion over your grandfather's burial."

Bianca blushed, hesitant to take the box. "No, I'm the one who should be sorry. I spoke to my gran and she told me that only the ashes were on the hillside. I had no need to search for bones." Bianca smiled, remembering the few times she had lugged pieces of bone back to her apartment only to find they were farm animals, probably killed years ago by marauding town dogs that often hunted in packs along the creeks of her childhood.

She took the box at his insistence, astounded and subdued by his thoughtfulness, although she was just a little cautious, secretly wondering if this was some kind of joke. Opening the lid slowly, she saw the pearly gleam of the little warrior perched on his piece of stone.

"You still have it. How much do you want for it?"

"It's a gift. It belongs to you now."

"No, no. I will pay you what it's worth. That's the reason I came to the market. Did you think I came back to visit you and get pushed into the mud?"

"Huh? No, I thought the warrior's spirit might drive you back here, so I wrapped him up and waited. Then the rains came, and I had almost given up seeing you again. But here you are, and now that we have solved some of our differences, I can ask you to dinner tonight."

"Why would I go to dinner with you?" Bianca asked, surprised by his invitation. She touched the smoothness of the statue and admired the artwork on the little, wooden box before glancing sideways at Jordan's face to check his sincerity.

"Well, we have a lot in common. I presume you are single. We have a shared ancestry and a rather odd interest in old bones. I am sure we will find a lot to talk about, and what better place to do it than down at the old pub over a good meal? My number's inside the box." Jordan handed her a plastic bag to protect his gift from the rain and then turned his attention to a customer who showed more than a passing interest in his resin and bone figures.

****

Bianca stepped lightly into the warmth of her apartment and unwrapped the warrior, setting the box and the statue on her windowsill where they would catch the light. The walk home had cleared her mind, and she realized that Jordan did not even know her name. She would call him immediately about returning the gift, angry with herself for even accepting it in the first place.

Bianca dialled the number, and Jordan's deep voice answered. Unprepared for a recorded message, she stumbled over her words, uncertain about what to say. "Hi, this is Bianca. I will be at the pub tonight at six thirty. See you then." She hung up, cursed her decision, and dialled again, intending to change the message. Before the recording had finished, Bianca hung up. She had said she'd be there and she would.

A pale beam of sunlight danced off the statue as Bianca skipped a few steps and smiled.

Mala

Mala lets her curly hair hang long. "It's messy," she says, but she doesn't really care, and the front bits are sun-bleached a kind of brassy colour like in those old photos of Indigenous children. She has brown skin weathered from spending hours outdoors with her horses. Mala has never been scared to get her hands dirty and will stop her car to pull a dead animal off the road. "It's dead," she says, "and won't feel anything if another car runs over it. But if we just leave it there, the eagles and hawks will have it for breakfast. That's OK too, but then they risk getting sideswiped by these massive trucks or hoons on their way to wherever."

She talks all the way to Bacchus Marsh. Her co-worker listens most of the time, but with Mala, you just learn to switch off. She won't mind and will keep talking even if you don't answer. Just a couple of kilometres from work, she grabs the wheel and demands that Kirsten stop the car.

"Echidna," she says, and she jumps out to do what she always does. The little animal lies on its back, legs in the air and its softer underbelly exposed to scavengers. Already the internal gases have started to swell the carcass so that it looks like a prickly piñata. She explores it gently with her toe, considering if there is a way to move it into the frosty, crisp undergrowth without actually touching the bloodied armour. Mala doesn't see a dark shape emerge from the bush until it is just metres from her and the spiny road kill. She hears a throaty growl, sees its yellow eyes, and spins around instantly, leaping back into the car and slamming the door. "Is that a dog or a cat?" she breathes and Kirsten looks back through the rear window, gasping at the sight of a sleek, black creature the size of a Rottweiler.

Then it is gone with the echidna dangling from its mouth by a leg. The two women just look at each other, Mala remaining silent for longer than is normal for her. "That's a story the boss will not believe," she says finally, and Kirsten slowly drives off with her eyes on the rear-vision mirror. But the animal is gone, and she wonders whether she has just imagined it as a giant cat.

Mala has no doubts. She finally finds her voice and says the echidna must have been fairly fresh because cats won't normally eat anything that's been dead for a while. It was swelling though, so maybe the beast had been really hungry. A lot of the native fauna had died or left the area during last summer's fires, so food might be scarce.

Kirsten sounds hesitant when she asks Mala if she really thinks it was a cat. "Can't be a cat," she says. "It was way too big. A dog maybe, but I have not heard of any wild dogs around here. And besides, it was too black and sleek for a dog."

Mala reminds her that they had been working in the forestry industry for years and had not seen anything like that before. But she says that there had always been stories about a panther let loose by American GIs after the war. Or was it a circus escapee like someone told her just a couple of years ago? She had not believed that there could be a giant cat out in the bush for all that time without somebody catching it in a trap. And besides, one cat could not live as long as the stories had gone around. There had to be more to it, or else it was just somebody's overactive imagination.

Kirsten says, "But that was real. We both saw a cat or something, and it was huge. Just don't say anything," she told Mala, "because it will start a hunt and cause all kinds of problems. We'll have thrill seekers tramping all over this bush, and besides, who will believe us anyway? Just don't tell anybody anyway because they will think we are crazy."

The two women look at each other, and Kirsten grips the wheel so hard her knuckles turn white and her eyes widen with something like fear. "I'm not scared," she says to Mala, "but that was really weird, and I don't think I just imagined it, did I?"

"Nah," Mala says. They both can't have imagined the same thing, and besides, there have been tales of wild panthers out here for yonks.

Mala reminds Kirsten that the old folk used to tell stories about some giant catlike creature back before white people came here. Of course, her ancestors didn't call them cats then, but some of the descriptions fit our version of feral felines, just larger. "Bunyips maybe," she says with a grin.

They drive the rest of the way in silence and feel rather relieved to be back in civilization. The town is icy and clothed in a thin veil of wood smoke from last night's fires. No wind has risen to drive the haze higher, and it will probably hang around all morning, increasing as townsfolk relight their Coonaras before work and school, so their houses will be cosy when they return at day's end. A faint smell of warm yeast pervades the air as local bakeries open their doors for the early risers. Sounds are muffled, and no birds call. A small dog yaps half-heartedly from behind the corrugated tin fence that separates the department buildings from old houses damp and dripping with morning dew.

Mala and Kirsten like getting to work early so they can enjoy a fresh coffee before the day's hard slog. If there is one thing that the department has in its favour, it's the coffee machine. The smell of fresh brew overpowers the mustiness of old files not yet relegated to online storage and lends warmth to cold corridors stacked ceiling high with excess furniture and archive boxes.

"We are not kids telling tales, you know," says Mala to her younger sidekick. "I'm nearly thirty and you aren't far behind me, so people will surely believe us." She paused, nursing the hot coffee mug before continuing. "Just in case though, we'll keep it quiet. If someone else reports this thing, then we will tell them what we have seen. Agreed?"

Kirsten says, "OK, Mala. What kind of name is that anyhow? Mala." As though she had never thought about it before or just needed something to take her mind off the morning's excitement.

"I don't know, except that my mum gave it to me when I was about two years old. My other name is Delia. She said I was like an overactive bush bunny and that she would name me after the little hare-wallaby that was always so fast and difficult to find, hiding in the scrub as it did. So she got Mala put on my birth certificate, and that made my old gran happy. She says that now I belong to the land where her parents used to hunt wallabies and dig for yams."

Kirsten is true to her word and says nothing about the apparition they saw in the bush. As the day wears on, she becomes less certain that what she saw was real and convinces herself that it was just a shadow. She asks Mala if they want to travel the main road home instead of risking another encounter, even though she probably imagined it all. Mala says, "Nah", they will just go the usual back way because she loves the bush in the evening and likes to watch the kangaroos loping out into the open grasslands for feed and hear the galahs screeching their goodnights.

Kirsten can drive, she says as she gets her camera ready just in case.

A winter sun sets behind them, lighting the topmost tips of eucalypts lush with new growth that erupted after the fires. Undergrowth on the roadsides has thickened since seasonal rains washed the ash and blackened soils into muddy watercourses sludging their way towards inland rivers. The bush seems alive with movement from a rising wind, and Mala puts her hand on Kirsten's arm, beckoning her to slow down where the morning's incident occurred. "There," she says. "Fresh kill. Wallaby hit by some idiot, and I hope his car was damaged. Payback for being careless."

Kirsten stops the car and pulls over so Mala can check if the animal is alive. "Don't get out," she says. "Just look through the window." Mala opens the window slightly and breathes in the sharp smell of eucalyptus.

"Should see if there is a young one in the pouch," Mala answers without moving. "Maybe we'll just wait a while and see if it comes back. Do you have to get home quickly for any reason?" Kirsten says it's OK, and her kids are with her mum for the night anyway. Mala says that this is a good story to tell them later, and kids always like a bit of a mystery.

She stiffens suddenly and whispers, "Look over there, behind that blackwood, in the dip just off the road. Don't move, and be quiet."

A black shadow seems to glide through the bush, even though there is no sun to cause a shadow and their car lights are off. Then there is nothing, and they sit in the cold silence, eyes strained to penetrate the falling darkness. A faint pinging sound drifts in from the front of the car, followed by the pungent smell of urine. Mala, open mouthed and wide-eyed, faces Kirsten, who is stifling a scream with shaky hands. Mala grins and silently mouths, "It's him. He pissed on our car!"

The shadow suddenly appears in the window behind Mala, so Kirsten keeps one hand over her mouth and jabs the air repeatedly with the other, soundlessly urging Mala to turn around. Mala barely catches a glimpse of the creature as she turns her head. The movement startles the animal. It slinks rapidly off into the darkness of the undergrowth. Gone in an instant, no time for photos, and the women are once again left doubting their own eyesight.

Within the hour, Kirsten is relieved to be back home in the doubtful security of their ever-expanding suburban community. She drops Mala off on the outskirts, where farmers have abandoned their weed-ridden paddocks to the money-hungry demands of city developers. It is just a short walk to the regenerated farmhouse she shares with her parents, and Mala feels again a sense of loss that intrudes on her usually carefree nature every time she passes the rows of new dwellings. Overpopulation, loss of wildlife habitats, and fertile farms being sold up for houses are her pet hates and the very reason she chooses to work so far from home, where people-free forests still exist.

The old weatherboard, painted in heritage colours of cream and green, is sandwiched between high fences and brick veneer units. Its wide verandah draped with deciduous vines offer some privacy from the neighbours' high windows. A welcoming smell of home cooking softens the claustrophobic effect Mala feels as she takes the steps two at a time to the front door. Her father is waiting and says that there was some news about a big cat in the forests up near the Marsh.

Mala pulls on her gumboots, tells her parents she will be back soon, and drives up the road to check on her horses. Lights from the newly constructed streets mean she does not need a torch anymore. She turns into a short, gravel driveway and leaves her car outside the tall, wrought-iron gates set deeply into a massive brick wall that surrounds the property. She has never been inside the fortress where the old lawyer and his wife lived, barricaded against their fears of Russian mafia. She follows the outside of the wall down to the open stables, checks the water trough, and spreads some straw in the sheltered bay where her horses will probably spend the cold night. Two ancient draught horses, left to fend for themselves when the old couple retired to the city, hang their heads in sleep, their breath forming a musty cloud in the pale streetlights. They stir and whinny gently as she enters the yard, welcoming company even this late in the evening. Soon their paddocks will be a subdivision, and they will be taken away. Mala shudders at the thought of them being used as fertilizer or pet food and tends her own horses, knowing that she will have to rehouse them farther out of town before the coming spring.

Retracing her steps along the wall, Mala thinks about the day's happenings and glances behind as night sounds and broken shadows seem to follow her. "Don't be silly," she admonishes herself, but she moves a little faster away from the dark mounds of rusted machinery and corrugated iron that harbour rodents unchecked by the local council. "We could do with a big cat here to keep the bunny population down," she whispers to herself as an innate fear threatens to destabilize her calm. Mala runs the last few metres to the gates, conscious of how foolish she is acting. As she reverses out the unkempt driveway, she hears the rustling of dried grasses and weeds under her car and sees little bats dart across the yellow lights, catching winged insects released by her wheels.

Spooked by the apparition she and Kirsten had seen that morning, Mala is relieved to see the glow of her father's cigarette in the dark recesses of the bull-nosed verandah. Normally, she would enjoy the evening chores, taking pleasure in the comparative silence of the paddocks and the horsey smell that pervades the old sheds and lingers on her clothes. Today is different, and she has difficulty in understanding her own reactions to the events.

"Do you think it's a cat?" he says quietly as he butts out the forbidden smoke in an old tin can. Without waiting for a reply, he says, "Dinner's ready, so we'll watch it on the news."

Mala's dad is brown and weathered, like her, from his days as a farmer. He had grown tired of defending his sheep from domestic dogs allowed to run wild by suburban owners who denied that their pets could ever be killers. The tense nightly vigil and the inevitable morning heartbreak when he would find lambs torn apart and ewes with their snouts ripped so badly he had to destroy them had taken a toll on his health.

Eventually, he stopped farming altogether and went to work at the airport as a cleaner. When new laws allowed subdivision, he sold his land, keeping the old house that has belonged to his family since before there was even a town. Animal regulations have tightened since then, and Mala wishes her father could have just waited a few more years before selling out to city developers. At least her horses are safe now from marauding canines. She thinks about the big cat and turns on the evening news.

She tells her parents that she saw the animal that morning scavenging road kill, but she agreed with Kirsten that they should keep it quiet. Her mum disagrees, but her dad says she is right. "It won't do to stir up trouble and have people pointing at you", he says. "You know that there are myths about cats that go way back, before my time even, and people will think that you are playing on the old stories, trying to get attention or something." Mala says, "Times have changed, and nobody thinks like that anymore. We can be whomever we want to be, excepting, of course, if we come off a boat."

He says he can see the headlines already. Indigenous forestry worker relives dreamtime stories. "We'll have the local paper ringing for an interview and readers abusing us for using the past to bring attention to ourselves."

"As if," Mala says. "Why would we want to bring attention to ourselves? Why would you worry anyway? And I hate the way people are labelled in the press. Like when they say, for instance, 'a grandfather killed in an accident' or 'a grandmother involved in some incident' when describing them as either a man or woman would be sufficient." Mala gets angry when she is labelled as Indigenous, even though she likes the fact that her ancestors were around before the tall ships entered the protected waters of Port Phillip Bay. She gets angry when her cousins visit and complain incessantly about inadequate welfare payments and their other entitlements that they deserve because they are first Australians. "Grow up," she says. "We are all Australians and should be treated equally. Handouts don't do anyone any good." She tells them that she got through uni and landed a great job without ticking the application boxes that would have allowed her special treatment as an Indigenous woman. They think she should stand up for her people more.

"It's just the way some people think," says Dad, "and others still put us down even though our family has been farming and living here since last century. Long before most of the residents of this town." He doesn't speak much about when his father's father came out as a convict and settled down with an Aboriginal woman, eventually earning the right to buy a parcel of land where houses now stand. She knew her grandfather in turn also married a woman from the fast-disappearing local tribe, ensuring that the bloodlines would continue into this generation. Her father believes in keeping the past in the past and not stirring up any controversy. "Better just to keep the cat story to yourselves," he says. "Shut your mouths, and avoid trouble."

Mala's mother looks at her own brown hands and says she doesn't understand why things should be so difficult anyway. She doesn't care what people think. Mala can't decide whether to keep the incident to herself or to tell the world, but there is one thing she knows for certain. She just doesn't want to stand out or be noticed as someone who is different. Tomorrow she will talk to Kirsten.

Early next morning, Mala leaves before her parents awaken. They have discarded the habits from their farming days and no longer worry about wasting time sleeping in. They spend long hours in the community veggie patch, and once a week join the coffee drinkers down at the fair trading café. Mala has difficulty understanding their new life and a recently acquired need to meet others like themselves. She repeats her thoughts out aloud as she walks to meet Kirsten on the main road out of town. "Others like themselves," she says. "What does that even mean, and what gives those people the need to think they are in any way different from the mainstream?" Mala finds it impossible to fathom why people fight for the right to be equal and then, when that is achieved, they want their difference acknowledged, drawing together in social groups of like-minded folks. Separate from the others.

A couple walking their dogs look at her, and she explains that she is just thinking out aloud. She is embarrassed but reassured as they call back to her that we all do that. *At least they said "we," which means they see us as the same as them,* Mala thinks as she waves cheerily while Kirsten's 4WD appears.

"Let's go chase up this big cat," she says with determination, "and who gives a shit what other people think?"

Kirsten knows the decision is final and is pleased to have the old, confident Mala back on track.

Ted

"You believe in aliens, Ted?"

"Dunno. And stop calling me shithead, arsehole."

"I didn't. I called you Ted."

"But I know what you meant. You can be a frickin' prick at times, Jimmy."

"So it's all right for you to call me names, but I can't even call you Ted? Anyway, your old man believes in all that alien stuff, doesn't he?"

"Yer. Says we were made by something from out there that came down and used artificial insemination on the apes to produce a human being. Says we evolved from that first human or humans. Like an avatar maybe."

"You're joking. Why artificial insemination?"

"Guess they couldn't do it the normal way. Anyway, don't ask me. I'm just tellin' it like my dad said."

"Hasn't he read the Bible? What about Adam and Eve and all that stuff?"

"Just a story. I don't believe in all that crap, and neither does my dad. He says there is a different explanation about our beginnings. Mentioned that we are the only earth race to wear clothes and drive cars. Funny though that all religions seem to kind of go back to one god, or being, that started it all. I think we just haven't grasped the idea, yet that there is something our brains simply aren't designed to see. Way beyond our pathetic comprehension or imagination. Preprogrammed by the aliens, my dad would say."

"Hang on a minute, Ted. Some of the monkeys and apes use leaves as blankets at night, or as rain hats. Doesn't that mean clothes? Anyway, clothes are part of the evolution process. Really though, I have my doubts about whether or not we descended from monkeys. I don't believe in all this religion shit either, but like you said, there is nothing else to help me understand our beginnings. Nothing *my* brain can visualize."

"Visualize? Do you even know what that word means?"

"Aw, c'mon. Just because I'm black doesn't mean I'm illiterate."

"You are a fuckin' actor, Jimmy. You're no blacker than me."

"You tell that to those guys down at Centrelink. I'm tellin' you, once you tick the right box, there's no escape. According to them, I'm black, and that means I'm slotted into all those special needs categories."

"Not what you want?"

"What d'ya reckon? How'd you be if everyone started calling you Prince Ted just because you have all that orange hair and expecting you to do royal things?"

"*Red* hair, and it's come from the Vikings, not the English."

"Ha! Even worse. How come I've known you since kindergarten, and you've never told me that before?"

"How come *you* never told me your grandparents were black, until you turned eighteen? Amazing what comes out when you are drunk."

"When was I ever drunk?"

"Jimmy, you are always drunk. Don't know why I ever hang around with you, me being a non-drinker and all."

"Pull the other leg, Ted. You keep tellin' people you don't drink, and yet you always have a red wine or two with your meals, and you can put away a few beers when the footy is on. It drives me crazy that you keep denying it."

"There's a few things you hide too, Jimmy. Like you keep sayin' that stuff about not being able to escape the labels that people put on ethnics, and yet I don't see you really trying. You like the idea of being black and are probably just angry that you aren't black enough. Isn't that right?"

"The hell with you. You've never understood. And anyway, we were discussing aliens, not earthlings."

"Changing the subject, are we? Start calling me by my proper name, and I might have a little more respect for your ideas, Jimmy. Look, I'll write it down for you so you don't forget. Jason, not Edward. Jason. Edward is my second name, and I am never Ted."

"You make it so complicated, Ted."

"You'll never learn, will you? And anyway, you can't scoff at my dad's theories when your old man believes in all that dreamtime stuff. I heard him talking down at the pub coupla months ago. Drunk as a skunk and telling us that we all came up from the centre of the earth, lived here for a while creating rivers and lakes and rocks and animals. Some stayed while the others went up into the sky and became the moon, stars, and stuff. Aliens of another kind. Or a different slant on the creation concept."

"Ahh. So you admit you *drink* at the pub. Lemonade, I presume. You obviously listened to my dad pretty hard because you remember it all. Can't deny that dreamtime stories have a basis. Look at all those rock drawings of Wandjina up north and the Yowie stories closer to home. Weird figures unlike any people we know. Not unlike your alien theories, are they?"

"They're not *my* theories, you frickin' idiot. Load of rubbish, I reckon. Mind you, Jimmy, I don't think our earthling brains, especially yours, are capable of getting away from all that, and it seems easier to believe in gods and aliens than to try to get our heads around some other kind of beginning. I doubt that we will ever know how we started, don't see anyone actually capable of thinking outside the old stories. Our brains just can't comprehend that any other form of life can exist. Something that our eyes cannot see either because we have tunnel vision when it comes to these things."

"You are right, Ted. You are always right. However, there's all those rock drawings. Weird figures and animals, symbols that have some forgotten meaning. Stories passed down through the generations that probably haven't changed for centuries. Still, stories do become warped as they are spoken from person to person, generation to generation, but the drawings haven't changed. Well, maybe they have, because as the nomads passed through they *may* have redone some of the graphics or added things to the meaning."

"Jimmy, just because there are drawings on rocks doesn't make it real. They just couldn't draw people as well as we can today because they lacked imagination, or proper tools."

"Ahh! You admit then that you think the original Australians lacked the imagination to *make up* these spacemen creatures. If they had no *imagination,* then they must have been copying from real-life incidents or memories. They probably actually *saw* some alien or godlike forms and drew them in the caves where they hid and where they could get the coloured ochres."

"This is goin' fuckin' nowhere. Just understand this: I don't believe in any of that crap. I'm an atheist. You can believe whatever you want, but don't try to convince me that I should go to church or bow down to cave paintings, or run out and photograph every strange thing I see in the night sky. Why the hell are we talking about this stuff anyway?"

"OK. OK. I only asked the question, Ted."

"What is it with you? Where is all this coming from?"

"Dunno. Just been thinking about things lately. About the past, you know, and how neither of us knows much about our family histories. And how we've been friends for a quarter of a century and yet we don't really know each other that much. Just work and football and the pub."

"Isn't that enough?"

"What about death? Do you ever think about what happens after we die?"

"Now, this is getting creepy. Are you OK, Jimmy, old pal?"

"Sure. Just thinking, Ted."

"And for the record, Jimmy, I believe that once we are dead, that's it. No more. Nothing. Gone forever. Remember that when you bury me."

Jimmy

I never really knew him. This is what I was told ...

Jimmy is a bachelor in his midthirties, tall, rugged looking with a swarthy complexion, and dark, wiry hair. He wears flannelette shirts with buttons missing and rolled-up sleeves. His skinny jeans are faded and have thin patches where his suntanned skin shows through. He lives alone in a heritage bungalow down by the creek, not far from the house that Jacob left when he moved to the nursing home.

He was a tradie, most times building concrete driveways and curbing in the new estates to the north of town. Sometimes when work was unavailable or union reps started hassling him about membership fees, he visited Centrelink and stood in the queue for what seemed like hours, comparing himself to others in the same situation. Except he felt different.

Generally, he avoided signing up for welfare and botted off his dad or sometimes his friends. Jimmy hated waiting for handouts, but most of all, he dreaded the questions that were asked of him. He left tick boxes empty, preferring not to answer some issues and waited for the inevitable response from impatient staff who could not see beyond the categories written in their mental handbooks.

The building was cool in both colour and climate, impersonal and with no decoration to make the wait more visually pleasant. Pale-green walls blended with the grey furniture and computer terminals. Nobody in the waiting queue spoke above a whisper so the voices at the reception desk seemed loud in comparison. Questions were amplified in the low-ceilinged office, making personal details available to other clients and staff. "When did you last put in a form, date of birth, reasons for applying? Do you have a doctor's certificate? Anything else you need to tell?" Always the same questions, delivered by rote without a smile, and Jimmy wondered if the interrogator *really* heard his answers or even cared what was asked.

Random thoughts from years past floated in and out of his head as Jimmy waited for the inevitable grilling.

He had left school after year twelve and decided to fill in a gap year working with seasonal fruit pickers across the nation. He found his way up north, travelling alone by bus when he could afford to and hitching rides at the local truck stops when his money ran out. Jimmy fitted in easily with the Indigenous folk he met along the way and hooked up with a couple of dark-skinned Queenslanders travelling free like himself. Their hands and fingernails were stained in dirty patches from banana harvesting or tomato picking, and within a few weeks, Jimmy proudly sported the same discoloration.

Late in the summer season, the pickers decided to take a break and head down to the beaches along the east coast south of Brisbane, where they could avoid the deadly marine stingers that swarmed along the shallow northern waters. Jimmy was invited but was short of cash, so the guys took him down to the dole office and helped him fill out the forms that might ease his travels. Money for nothing, they said.

For a gullible eighteen-year-old, that sounded pretty good, and they told him he was entitled to some money because he had been working so hard and everyone deserved a holiday. The guys ticked all the boxes for him, including the one where he identified as an Aboriginal. Looking back, he believed they simply did what they had always done for their own identification and was appreciative that they considered him one of their mob. But they should have asked.

An irritable girl behind the counter had not been interested in verifying any of the details and seemed rather anxious to rid the office of noisy out-of-towners and seasonal pickers. Jimmy gave the Brisbane address of an accommodating cousin of one of the travellers. His dole would be through in a few weeks, and in the meantime, he was able to collect some hardship money. Jimmy never understood the process or the outcome, but neither did he doubt that it was legitimate. Only years later did he realize his identity had been recorded and categorized, his individuality taken.

Nowadays, back home in a town where everybody knows everybody else's business, Jimmy is embarrassed to ask for welfare. He finds the new forms more difficult and knows there will be interrogation and plenty of awkward suggestions that he was able to avoid all those years ago. When his number comes up, he leans into the cubicle at the counter, keeping his voice low and trying to gain some privacy behind the laminated partitions. Always the same, but until recently, Jimmy had managed to see beyond the dark clouds of doubt and stay calm, feigning a casualness that he hoped would fool those he had to face on a daily or weekly basis.

Then things became too difficult, and he began to lose the control he had exercised in the past. That autumn, something changed. This was a season that often revived feelings and memories from his youth, when the shorter days and still balmy evenings gave Jimmy and his friends an excuse to walk through the leaf-littered park to the pub, skylarking like children along the way. Now the pleasure had gone.

There was no point anymore in pretending that things were normal, and an incident at the dole office made him question his own sanity. When his number was called, Jimmy felt an inexplicable panic rising from his stomach and exploding silently in his head. When he approached the desk, a pony-tailed man behind the counter asked him to speak louder and pointed to the unticked boxes on the form. He said impatiently that Jimmy must answer *all* the questions, including where it asks if he is Aboriginal or Islander. Jimmy explained that he had already filled the section that says he is an Australian citizen, and that should be sufficient. His ancestry was really none of their business, and if his friend Jason had never been required to explain where his grandparents originated, why should he?

The clerk glanced irritably at a large railway clock ticking on the pillar behind him. Newspaper clippings, family photos, and yellow sticky notes had been taped untidily beneath the clock, their edges curled and discoloured over time, their meanings forgotten as staff relocated to other sections or suburbs. A typed memorandum, in bold print, asked that reception staff ensure clients complete their forms correctly and tick all the required boxes. Another handwritten message requested that people who used the improvised notice board clear away out-of-date and unwanted data as soon as possible.

Unwanted data. The irony was not lost on Jimmy. He reread the parts on the form that he had neglected to fill and quietly told the clerk that although this stuff was personal and unnecessary, he would do as he was asked. To the question of whether he was Aboriginal or Torres Strait Islander, he answered in the negative and handed the form back.

After a pause, the clerk pointed to the offending box and said that this was not what they had on their records and asked if Jimmy was sure he wanted to answer that way. Jimmy seemed calm and explained that he did not wish to be labelled. He just wanted to get a bit of money so he could go out and find another job. A supervisor was called in while the waiting queue became restless, murmuring distractedly amongst themselves and pacifying bored toddlers with packets of salty nibbles and grubby plastic toys.

Jimmy was nervously concerned that his mismatched answers would be considered fraud, but he was tired of being asked the same questions that are on record anyway. If he answered something different with each regrettable visit, he risked getting their unwanted attention, but he felt a need to clear a few cobwebs. And besides, he considered himself as Australian and didn't feel guilty about rejecting his heritage. Jimmy preferred to live in the present, seeing no need to use a past that never really belonged to him anyway. Lately though, the past seemed to be intruding on his daily life, creating complications that he found difficult to handle.

The clerk asked him to wait a minute while he spoke to his supervisor. A chubby woman with red cheeks and a startled expression checked the answers, occasionally glancing at Jimmy sandwiched between the partitions, elbows on the counter and clasped hands holding up his unshaven chin. Jimmy kept eye contact as long as he could, trying to look knowledgeable as though he understood everything they argued about. In reality though, their forms and their reasoning were foreign to him, and he cared little for the legalities behind their methods of questioning.

The assistant returned to the counter and again asked Jimmy if those were the answers he wanted on his record. He said the supervisor needed to know why personal details had changed and asked if he was rejecting his Aboriginality. Jimmy put his hands in his pockets so the assistant could not see that he was making a tight fist. If his hands were loose, he might just have been tempted to use them. He kept his outward calm and assured the clerk that he had answered the questions correctly. That was what he wanted.

He was told that he must make another appointment to clarify the issue and ensure that no mistakes were made that might jeopardize future transactions. Jimmy did not move for a few seconds, and then he placed his hands on the counter and put pressure on his fingertips until they turned white. His jaw was clamped shut, and he knew that if he spoke he would say something that he would later regret. He saw the security guards two cubicles down to the right, although they had not noticed him yet. A sound issued from behind his teeth as he sucked in air, and he could no longer remain indifferent. He thumped his fists against the partitions and tore up the paperwork, quietly but savagely telling the assistant that the form was correct and that all he needed was money to survive and to search for a better job.

Jimmy left before the guards began to move towards him, striding quickly through the first of the sliding doors and waiting for them to close before he pressed the button to open the second set that would release him into the dusty, leaf-strewn street. He felt angry with the assistant, angry with himself for not controlling his temper, and most of all, he was angry at a system that refused to accept him as he was, without hang-ups or tags that differentiated him from others.

Things have become worse since Jason died, his body lost somewhere off wind-whipped rocks where wild southern seas spoiled their annual fishing venture. Jimmy had not wanted to go but Jason, or Ted as he knew him, had usually been the decision maker, and this occasion was no different. Jason always had a way of putting Jimmy back in his box without jeopardising a friendship that had only briefly been broken when Jimmy travelled north. That trip had left good memories and Jimmy did consider doing a rerun, but there were things in this town that needed sorting out first. His family was here, and there was a girl who showed some interest in him. There was a mortgage to pay, and he could not leave his ageing dog. Always there was some reason for delaying any change in his lifestyle.

Recently, with Jason gone, Jimmy had become even more entrenched in the monotony of regional life and retreated into the security and isolation afforded by his quarter acre down near the creek. He found it difficult to get out of bed in the mornings, and there were always aches and pains that prevented him from working. The days seemed long, and television held no interest; the summer months brought little joy, and winter's black clouds echoed his own deep feelings of sadness. Jane, the girl who had often stayed overnight, called in less frequently and told him she wanted the other Jimmy back, the one who laughed and treated her with such gentleness. She did not like this new Jimmy who slept for days on end and forgot to shower or to feed his dog. Eventually, she took the animal home with her and refused to bring him back. Jimmy hardly noticed him missing until several weeks had passed and he could no longer use the dog as a pretext for staying home.

Still, he found excuses to avoid work. When the money ran out, so did his appetite. Food seemed unnecessary and a bother to prepare. Jane brought him ham sandwiches or baked pasta in reused microwaveable cartons left over from her own takeaways. She noted the deterioration in the house. She told him to get off his backside and clean the place up a bit, that Jason was not coming back and he must accept that things had changed. A storm sparked and darkened in his brain, and he lashed out at her comments, pushing her from the house and slamming the door. Jimmy was overcome with a sense of loss that seemed to begin long before Jason disappeared, and he could no longer hold back the emotion that had threatened to destabilize him for the past weeks, months, and even years.

Confusion addled his brain, and he relied more and more on the generosity of his dad. Jane tried to find answers to this change in his character and comforted him when he was receptive. The other times she left him alone to stew in his own deepening sadness and knew that she could not spend her life sorting out other people's problems. Jimmy sheltered behind his own thoughts and waited in bed for someone to visit. He heard the mailman stop at the end of his driveway but could see no point in collecting any more bills and overdue notices when he had no money to pay them anyway. Envelopes and junk mail spilled out onto a garden overgrown with sticky weed and dandelions. Jimmy's father gathered the soggy papers and sorted out the ones he recognized. The others he left unopened, stacked on the doorstep for his son to collect. He settled some bills and waited for the day when the bank lost patience over Jimmy's unpaid mortgage. There was a limit to his hard-earned finances now that he had retired, but he did whatever he could. Money seemed to be a minor problem though, compared to his son's mental state.

Jimmy saw the anguish in his dad's eyes whenever he visited. He tried to explain, but there was no reasonable explanation. He didn't know why he felt so muddled but saw that Jason's death was the trigger for a sense of unreasonable resentment that had existed deep inside his psyche since he'd left school. Overlapping thoughts just kept welling up in his brain, and while a part of him desperately wanted friends and family around, there was always an inexplicable fear that made him lock the door against visitors.

Bear went to the door some time ago and ignored Jimmy's request to go away. Casual, placid Bear lived without seeing the complications in life that others created for themselves. When he found the door locked, he went around through a side gate and hoisted his giant frame through a window that he knew was always jammed open. The window had never been repaired because Jimmy said it was his insurance, an escape route against fire, intruders, or lost keys.

The wide, wooden sill cracked under Bear's weight and splintered to the ground just as he dropped shoulder first to the cold, white tiles on the kitchen floor. He remembered climbing through that same window as a teenager, when the house lay empty and local kids used it as a meeting place. Back then, the floors were littered with possum droppings and discarded food wrappers. Bear noted that not much had changed as he surveyed the downward deviations in cleanliness that had occurred since his last visit. Jimmy had always been a stickler for tidiness since he had renovated the old house ten years back, but his escalating illness had recently prevented him from keeping up the maintenance.

While Bear stepped carefully across the floor, Jimmy appeared silhouetted in the doorway to the lounge, his thin body partly dissolved into the light behind and his long arms apparently floating by his side. Alien like. Bear was never much for talking, so when Jimmy accused him of trespassing and yelled at him to get out, Bear simply shrugged and headed for the door. Without warning, Jimmy rushed at him, shoving him angrily into the hallway. Bear shook himself free and turned to face the now irate Jimmy, pinning his arms against the wall. He had never seen Jimmy in this state and was certain that something had snapped in his brain. Pushing hard with his hands and shoving his knee into Jimmy's stomach, Bear gruffly managed to ask what he was on about, and had he been taking anything? Jimmy had always been equal to Bear in physique and strength, but the past months had taken their toll and his deprived body no longer had the capability of fighting back. Frustration made him angrier, and he refused to give in, yelling and accusing Bear of intruding. One thing about Jimmy that had made him stand apart from his concreter mates was his ability to control his language, no matter what the company or the situation. Now, pinned against the plaster that he had so painstakingly restored when he bought the house, obscenities streamed from his mouth and shocked Bear into releasing him. He was certain that Jimmy needed more help than he could provide, and he started to phone for help. Jimmy knocked the mobile from his hands and threw a few wild punches, not caring where they landed. Bear reeled and hit the floor hard as Jimmy caught him on the side of his head. He lay there more surprised than in pain and suffered a few kicks in his ribs before Jimmy fell to his knees, physically and mentally exhausted by the sudden, uncontrollable onslaught.

Bear hesitated, but when he saw the tears and heard the moans, he knew that something had to be done immediately. With his arms around Jimmy's shoulders, he knelt close to his friend and called Jane. She found them a half hour later, seated cross-legged on the cold floor, silent and still, their knees barely touching and their eyes lowered. *Two unsmiling black Buddhas*, she thought, not daring to voice her reaction for fear of upsetting Jimmy again. She could not understand the hang-ups he had about his heritage and doubted that Jimmy could explain even if he wanted to.

Nobody knew much about what happened after that incident. It seemed that Jimmy did get some help, but he never really recovered. People tended to put his problems in the "too hard basket" and hoped that things would pass without their help. Some blamed it on his background, and others on Ted's untimely death. His parents also came in the firing line with counsellors trying to tell them that they should encourage Jimmy to be proud of his heritage. They asked, "Which heritage are you talking about? Why did he have to choose? Why did he have to be treated differently?"

Jane eventually moved in with him, the dog died, and she moved out again, unable to cope with his mood swings. Last week, he was still there in the house by the creek. Things had been tidied and the paint had been refreshed, but the neighbours rarely saw him and he didn't go into the town much anymore. His dad still visited, but their relationship was not what it used to be, and Jimmy blamed him for the confusion that still dwelled deep in his mind. Jimmy was not sure where his place in this town, in this society, in the minds of the people, belonged. He felt different and could not explain why. Despite that, it seemed he was recovering, or at least his friends and family liked to think so. He lived on his disability allowance, slept for days at a time, and worked on his house during the waking periods. Jimmy refused to take his medication for reasons he kept to himself and survived on Vegemite sandwiches washed down with soda water.

I heard about his accident from Jane, who had stoically remained his friend through the hard times. She found herself another guy not so long ago, but the romance was short-lived. It seemed that Jane was attracted to people with problems, and when he started pushing her around, she said enough is enough and dropped him immediately, only afterwards confiding in her long time friend who lived in the grey clouds of depression. Jimmy was surprised by her need to know other people, having been insulated for so long from the personal feelings of others. He dwelled within his own raging insecurities and felt betrayed by the knowledge that Jane had been with someone else, even though their own relationship had amounted to nothing more than friendship since he went off the rails.

Jane was the one who found him lying in the bathroom, empty pill bottles and sachets strewn across the vanity unit. She quickly covered his skinny frame with the towels and tried to scream for help. No sound would come, as her instinct was to close her mouth against the nauseating stench of vomit. She grabbed a pillow from the bedroom, placed it under his head, and frantically called for an ambulance. Her voice was punctuated by stops and starts, but she managed to tell them somehow that he was still warm and that she could not hold back her own spew much longer and had to leave the room.

She said it was strange how the mind worked in a crisis. While she was avoiding looking at Jimmy, she saw and remembered items on the crumpled doona and the dresser in the bedroom. She saw the didgeridoo that he had bought all those years ago in Queensland and the old photos of his Indigenous friends strewn across his pillow. She saw one of Jason, his red hair combed into an Afro, and one of herself, both torn down the middle.

She says that luckily, or unluckily, depending on which way you look at it, Jimmy didn't swallow enough and survived. He now lies in a hospital bed unaware of what is going on around him. Jane visits, but she was hurt and confused by the ripped photos and angry with Jimmy for being so selfish. Bear comforts her and does his best to hold a conversation with his comatose friend.

He wonders if perhaps Jimmy had always been that way and they just hadn't noticed.

Andrew

Andrew loved the half-light of early morning. He feared the dark nights, and the long days were wrought with anguish, but that lonely time in between gave him sanctuary. He wandered the scrubby land between the town and the tip, listening to the bell miners calling in the new day and watching cockatoos take flight across an orange-tinted sky. He smelled the wattles and searched in vain for frogs that once inhabited a creek now fed by oily drains and street run-off.

Andrew was small for his age. Mostly, he foraged whatever he could from the pantry and ate nothing at school. Sometimes, his dad would buy fish and chips before he went to the pub. Andrew relished the crisp, salty taste and afterwards sucked on the piece of lemon tucked away in the corner of the box. Weekends, there would be a barbecue with some of his dad's mates around for a free beer and plenty of sausages to fill his empty stomach. It didn't matter if there were no formal mealtimes because Andrew remembered the bad days before his mother left, when he and his brother had to sit straight at the table and eat every morsel without gagging.

"Sit still, and act civilized!" the old man would yell, his words slurred and threatening. "Not like your monkey mama over there. She never learned any manners because her dad never belted her enough. Now it's up to me to teach you all a few things and make you appreciate what you've got." Often, he would forget his own lessons and take his plate and his beer into the lounge where he would slouch in an old recliner, mumbling sourly, "That's what you get when you shack up with a boong."

His mother had gone one morning, taking the youngest child with her and leaving Andrew to celebrate his sixth birthday alone with his dad. It wasn't so bad while his father had regular work and the house was empty during the day. Andrew would tidy the dishes and get himself off to school, polishing his shoes like his mom had taught him.

Those times when the jobs dried up and his father slept in, he had to be quiet for fear of a thrashing. The house was no longer a refuge, and Andrew began to wander, leaving early and returning from school when the sun was low on the hills.

Usually, he would enter the house silently through the back door and curl up under his doona, hungry and still in his school clothes, waiting anxiously for the inevitable onslaught. Nighttime offered no respite. Andrew would often be dragged from his sleep because the washing was still on the line, the rubbish hadn't been put out, or—worse still—one of his dad's cronies needed a bed.

As he grew older, Andrew increased the range of his wandering. Sometimes, as he passed the local shops on his way to the reserve, he would collect a free bun from the bakery van or banana milk from the dairy truck. The drivers knew him and tousled his already unruly hair with hands that smelled of coffee and doughnuts, greeting him with mock warnings about wagging school and getting them in trouble for their generosity.

Munching happily, he would follow the concrete bike paths down towards school and then veer off into the remnant bush lands, pushing his way through patches of wild clematis and chocolate lilies. He was careful not to play truant too many days in a row in case his absence was reported to the principal or—worse—to his father. Sometimes, he would just disappear after first class, leaving his bag in the locker, and return at lunch break or the end of day.

Andrew had a few friends in secondary school that tried to tempt him with their unwanted apples or crunchy muesli bars.

"I'm just going to chuck it in the bin if you don't take it, 'cos if I bring it home, Mum will yell at me for not eating my lunch," they would say, unaware of the real reasons for his apparent lack of appetite but concerned enough to forgo their own munchies.

"Nah, that's OK. I don't like to eat in the middle of the day. Spoils my chicken tonight." Andrew would laugh and look away, in case the embarrassment showed in his eyes.

At thirteen, he had perfected the art of deception and kept his private life secret, never inviting friends home or joining in their weekend tomfooleries. He was quiet and likeable, but that didn't stop the bullies.

Fat Sam was on his second attempt at year eight and lorded it over the younger boys, especially Andrew with his dark hair and deep-brown eyes that told of a different heritage.

"You a blackfella, eh? Heard your mum took one look at you and ran off. Didn't want a throwback, eh?" Sam looked to his mates for support, relishing their sniggers and rude signs, pushing Andrew to respond.

Andrew's friends didn't like Sam or his comrades and could not understand why he just accepted the torments without some form of retaliation. "They are just words," he would say, shrugging his shoulders. "And he's the one with the problems, not me."

They weren't to know that the tears would wait for the dark of night when his dreams were punctuated by moments of waking fear and visions of his mother retreating from verbal blows that secured her silence.

"They are just words," she would whisper to him behind closed doors. "Your father has a problem. It's not our fault, and if we keep quiet, we won't get a belting."

One day, he would find her and tell her it was OK, he understood why she left and that he has tried to do what she taught him. He would not tell her that he pocketed a mandarin or kiwi fruit as he sidled past the neatly packed fruit stalls taking up space on the pavement in the town centre. Or about the supermarket where sliced-cheese sachets slipped neatly into the ill-fitting sleeves of his school spray jacket. Even his friends did not notice, being too preoccupied with choosing their favourite brands of energy drinks or blueberry muffins.

The first time had been the hardest. Breaking the twin tubs of yogurt apart, pretending to search the middle shelves then bending lower so his jacket draped over the separated item. Whisking it into his inside pocket and then continuing the search, as though he could not find what he was looking for.

A young packer in his refrigerator coat asked him if he needed help. Andrew was quick to answer, giving an absurd reason for his apparently fruitless search. "My friends said there was a new peanut-butter yogurt just come out, so I wanted to try one. But I can't find any."

The assistant laughed. "I think your mates have been messing with your brain, kid. Peanut-butter? That's a new one."

He delved in his pockets and handed Andrew a plastic spoon. "Here, take this. Now you go out there and find your mates, tell them you found the yogurt, ate it all on the spot because it was so delicious, and then stick the spoon in your mouth as evidence."

Andrew stood there breathless for a moment then thanked the young man and hurried to the entrance. He felt tears welling in his eyes and kept his head low, trying to appear calm as he left the store. Guilt overwhelmed him as he held his arms close by his side, pressing the cold tub against his thin shirt, its sharp edges prickling into his skin just below his ribs.

Things got easier after that, and he learned to avoid the aisle of snack foods where other kids hung out and where staff kept a close watch on their movements. He learned the best time of day to shop and supplemented his pilfering with tasty, cooked on the spot, samples handed out by visiting salespeople. When they explained that they were not allowed to serve kids without their parent's permission, Andrew cheerily dashed off, returning within seconds to say it was OK because he had asked his mum.

He never visited the same supermarket too many times in a month and sometimes avoided them altogether. It all depended on how sober his dad had been and how well he had stocked the pantry. Shopping with his dad was the best time to fill his pockets. He simply followed the old man through the checkout, helping unload groceries from the trolley and mentally willing staff to ignore the bulk in his coat sleeves. At home, he would hide the stolen goodies in an empty space beneath the bottom drawer of his old bedside table. Next to the worn photographs of his mother and the brother he hardly knew.

Still, he sought the silence and safety of those early mornings before his shadow showed on the damp grass and dilapidated paling fences along the reserve. Often, he would put his eye to a gap between the boards and watch the lights go on in the houses. He saw the families silhouetted behind flimsy blinds and smelled toast cooking for the children that he imagined climbing out of rumpled beds, sleepy eyed and warm. If he was lucky, he might see cats or dogs released happily into the garden for their morning play or toilet break.

It was on one of those mornings that he was caught. A walker with his yellow-eyed kelpie saw Andrew pressed against the fence and yelled questions at him. "Hey! What are you doing looking over my fence, young fella?"

Andrew froze momentarily, feeling the dog's hot breath on his bare knees. He could not run, having learned over the years that punishment was better taken in the instant he was caught. If he escaped, the ongoing anguish would be relentless, as he knew that penalties doubled with time.

"Answer me. What are you doing spying on my family? Are you some kind of pervert?"

He was a big man with worker's hands, calloused and darkened from manual labour. Bigger than his father, angry and red-faced from the intrusion into his private life.

"I know you. I've seen you round these parts before. What's your name, kiddo?"

Andrew just shook his head and began to hoist his schoolbag back onto his shoulders. He understood enough to know that this man could not legally restrain a child, but they were alone in the reserve and there would be no witnesses. Andrew tried to explain that he just wanted to see the happiness in someone else's family, to feel the warmth of eating breakfast together and to watch children unafraid of making mistakes that would be punished. The words would not come, and he mumbled an apology about not perving, just looking.

"Not good enough, fella. I will be going to see your teachers about this, and I am sure they will let your parents know what you have been up to. Anyway, what kid goes to school at this hour? The sun is barely up, and not only that, you're headed in the wrong direction. You're wagging school, aren't you?"

Andrew was released from the man's questioning, his knees shaking and his throat dry with fear. He headed back towards the school, his mind going over and over the incident that would ultimately be reported to his father. He searched for excuses that would go unheeded anyway and prepared himself for the inevitable.

True to his word, the man fronted up to school reception that same day, putting in a complaint about the kid who could become a problem as he grew older, spying on women and children in their own backyards. His actions should be nipped in the bud right now and his parents told. "If his parents have any problems with my report, tell them to come and see me, Joe Camilleri, and I will give them a piece of my mind for letting that peeping-tom skip school just to gratify his sick fantasies."

The matter did not end there. Word spread around the school, and eventually the principal caught up with Andrew, recognizing him from Joe's description and from Sam's malicious rumours.

"You understand I must talk to your father, Andrew. Can you explain why you have been leaving the school grounds without permission? And can you explain why you were eavesdropping on Mr. Camilleri's family?"

"No, sir. I wasn't wagging that day. I just decided to go for a walk before school. There was a hole in the fence, so I decided to look through. I like to look in other people's gardens and see if they have pets. I like the dogs, especially when they lick my fingers through the holes. I wasn't spying."

Andrew looked down at his shoes, the stitched edges frayed and the laces shortened from wear. The principal had already noted the high polish that was unusual for a student at his college. It did nothing to disguise the poor state of the shoes. He saw the uniform, thin and far too small, but clean and tidy, the socks with holes that showed above his shoes, and Andrew's, long, wiry hair, which showed some attempt at styling.

He had never really noticed the boy before, even though the school had fewer than three hundred students, and felt there was something amiss. Andrew's body language gave nothing away, no clue as to why he had behaved in this manner. Yet there was a sense that fear played a part in this boy's life.

The principal decided to look into the matter more deeply and to have the school counsellor involved.

Despite his concerns, or because of them, he had a duty to call Andrew's father. That same day, Andrew snuck down the side driveway at home, his feet making little sound on the rough gravel and his hands holding the zippers on his schoolbag to prevent them from clanging. He thought he could make it through the back door without his father knowing and was startled to find the old man waiting for him.

"What the fuck have you been up to?" His father roared angrily from the doorway, grabbing Andrew by the shirtfront. He threw the boy onto an old sofa that sufficed as outdoor furniture on the verandah. A loose spring jabbed into Andrew's lower back and his head hit the hard wooden arm where the stuffing had been clawed out by possums or stray cats. Dazed and trying to sit upright, he had time to see his father lurch towards him. He ducked low, tripping his father as he scrambled through his legs. He discarded his bulky schoolbag as he tumbled down the wooden steps, scraping his shins and knuckles against a rusty container of empty cans.

Andrew expected to be grabbed from behind before he reached the weedy lawn, but nothing happened. There was silence. He turned his face as he attempted to stand, considering running back down the drive and out onto the road.

He saw his father fall in slow motion from the couch onto the stained and splintered decking, his arms loose and his eyes rolling back to show the whites. Andrew stood unmoving for several moments, watching blood ooze gently from a gash on his father's forehead. He saw a bright stain on the brick window ledge behind the couch where his father must have hit his head, and he waited for the howl of pain and anger that would follow.

Nothing. The old man lay there motionless, and Andrew edged closer. He knelt beside the limp body, watching the lips turn blue and the breath coming in stops and starts. Andrew hesitated calling an ambulance, even though he knew that was the right thing to do. Delicious thoughts raced through his mind about the possibility of his father dying and where he would go if that happened. He knew that he was not old enough to live by himself and would probably end up in a foster home. Or maybe the authorities would contact his mother and bring her back to this town. That thought made him watch the bloodied face more closely, and he breathed a death wish into the rapidly darkening evening. He waited a few moments more before picking up his dad's mobile phone, dialling slowly and hoping that the ambulance would be delayed.

Andrew told them his father had tripped over some stuff left on the verandah, hitting his head on the sill and then falling onto the floor. He said that when he ran to help his dad, he also fell over, scratching himself on the container and bruising his cheek on the steps.

Within a few days, the old man recovered, releasing himself from the hospital and returning to his life of beer and crappy television shows. For a while, he did not have the strength to confront his son about either the incident or the school principal's concerns over voyeurism. Nobody seemed to notice the cuts and bruises Andrew had sustained, and he disguised them as best he could beneath long pants and an ill-fitting windcheater that covered his wrists.

A social worker had found him temporary accommodation while his father was hospitalized and later called by the house to check that he was managing with meals and washing. It was not long before the usual daily routine resumed and Andrew began to leave the house for longer periods. He avoided the reserve and occasionally spent time at a friend's place, relishing the feel of family living with sugary cupcakes and syrupy fruit juices that slid like velvet down his throat.

Fat Sam had been caught out, and the teachers gave Andrew more attention, apparently newly aware of the accident and the irresolute home situation. Despite that knowledge, nobody did much to help and left him in the care of his father. The small-town syndrome appeared to be alive and well in this village regardless of the expanding population and a rapid transition from rural living to city suburb. People preferred to mind their own business and let others sort out their own domestic problems. Andrew had been raised in this environment. He was one of them and kept his concerns private.

As soon as he was old enough, Andrew signed up for jobs in those very supermarkets that had sustained him through his early teens. Working after school and weekends meant he earned enough to buy an old bike that he hid from his father behind the back shed. His dad rarely ventured that far into the back yard, and Andrew had often secreted found treasures under the stacks of old palings and boxes now overgrown with sweet-scented jasmine and rampant ivy.

The bike gave him a freedom he had not previously known, and he was able to explore new areas outside the town boundaries, building his muscles and his mental resilience as he pushed through the hills and farmed flats. Andrew would always be small, but he grew stocky and strong, easily outrunning his father on those days when taking the punishment was not an option. His father could see the physical strength building and began to recognize something else in Andrew's dark eyes. And he wondered at his own fear.

The boy struggled through his final school year and increased his hours at the supermarket, eventually taking on a full-time roster. He rode his bike on weekends and occasionally partied with friends celebrating their end of school autonomy. Andrew avoided his father, tidying the house during the quiet hours when his old man was at the pub and relishing his newfound culinary abilities. He would often leave a homemade pasta or beefy pie on the bench for his dad, not expecting, or wanting, any thanks or appraisal.

The offerings were Andrew's way of easing his own guilt over the accident. It wasn't the accident itself or even his father's injuries that concerned him, but his own violent thoughts. He recalled the fear that had filled his heart that ill-fated evening and his intentional delay in seeking help. He had willed his father to die and now wondered whether that had anything to do with the old man's increasingly poor health. Was it possible that someone could be harmed by the evil mind processes of others? He questioned his friends, making a joke of the subject, and searched the local library for stories of bone pointers and kurdaitcha men. He wondered whether his mother had been able to leave him because she knew of his powers, then shook his head and told himself not to be so stupid. There were no powers, just coincidence and the passing of the years.

At eighteen, Andrew dreamed about a new life somewhere else but faced the reality with resentment. His father's needs had increased as his physical and mental capacity deteriorated. Andrew was tied to his home as a part-time carer still suffering verbal abuse, although he had no fear of being beaten. Now he could dish out the punishment, leaving his parent without meals, unplugging the television knowing his dad could not reach down to the power point and locking the doors behind him as he went to work. He would not have the privilege of escape that his son had known as a child, where the bush lands and reserves provided solitary respite.

To Andrew, his father had always been an old man, but now he saw the frailty and the listlessness, the transparent skin and the shuffle when he walked. He felt no sympathy, counting the weeks, the days that edged him closer to the time when he could put his father in a nursing home and have the house to himself. He checked the paperwork dumped in boxes throughout the house, looking for mortgages, title deeds, and insurances. He sifted through the stacks of envelopes and unopened mail, chucking whatever he could in the bin, taking pleasure in reducing his father's life to the few papers that would benefit his own future.

Andrew had not counted on the legalities, the difficulties he would have with the respective departments and the cost of a family lawyer. There were signatures required, and his father had to agree, unless, of course, he was considered incapable of making his own informed decisions. Finding a home with vacancies, deciding whether to put the house on the market or fight for the right to keep it, and convincing his father that there was no other way made Andrew even more indifferent to the old man's needs.

It was all too hard. Andrew continued to work long hours at the supermarket before going home to cook and clean. He had taken control of the house and of his father's life. The old man still was relegated to his bedroom where a timeworn TV had been installed, and he only felt free to wander the house while his son was at work. His mates from the club rarely called by, and loneliness filled his days. He began to believe that a nursing home would be a relief, and shortly before his seventieth birthday, he had made a decision.

"Andy, I've decided to sell up and move into a home. It'll be easier on you, and you can get on with your life."

Andrew was taken aback by this apparent show of consideration and for a moment said nothing. Then he realized that the sale of the house at this stage would leave him with nothing, nowhere to go, and only the nursing home would benefit from the extra money.

"You can't sell. I need this house."

"You and your bloody needs." His father's language and tone of voice reverted to the old days and reminded Andrew of the dread that had once ruled his life. "You can go and live with your bloody mother. It's about time she took some interest in your bloody life instead of leaving me to pick up the pieces."

"That was years ago, and you never told me where she had gone."

Andrew answered quietly, but his father saw the gritted teeth and the fists tightening by his side. He saw again the darkened eyes that had instilled inexplicable fear many times since the night of the accident.

"Where did she go?" Andrew asked suddenly. "Do you know where she is? Tell me where she is now, before I tell you what I am going to do with you."

His calmness was disquieting. The old man backed away a few steps, coming up against the kitchen table and falling uncomfortably into a chair.

Andrew moved a few steps closer, asking questions his father did not want to answer. "Why did you treat Mum so bad? My brother was just a baby, and yet you belted him as well. Why didn't she take me with her? Where is she, Dad? Did she really leave, or did you do something to her?"

"What? Do you think I've buried her in the backyard or something? Don't be so stupid. Your mum left because she was weak, because she didn't want us—me and you—anymore. She didn't want us," he repeated loudly, "so get that through your bloody thick head." The old man was trembling with anger, his hand shaking the beer loose from the can, spilling it in his lap and onto the floor. He started to stand up without his stick, and then he slipped on the wet tiles, hitting his head on the table and scooting the chair backwards as he went down.

Andrew froze. For a few seconds, he seemed to be a child again, back on the verandah, his father lying unconscious while he hesitated calling for help. This was the same situation, playing with his mind, giving him the chance to make a different decision. He turned slowly and, not looking back, went down the hallway and out through the front door. Calmly, methodically, he took his helmet from the front handlebars of his bike, strapped it loosely under his chin, and slowly wheeled out onto the street.

Andrew headed for the shopping centre where acquaintances and workmates would see him. For despite the population surge in this once quiet town, it was still small enough for people to recognize the regulars, and for once, Andrew wanted to be noticed. He parked his bike on the rack outside the sports store, locking the front wheel to the back of a bench. He removed his helmet and yawned, casually flinging his bag onto his back, before heading to the food court to collect cheap packaged meals left after the day's trading. Andrew loved cooking for himself but occasionally bought pasta or fried rice that could not be kept by the traders for another day. His father criticized these "foreign" foods but never hesitated to devour his portion with gusto.

An hour or two passed before Andrew decided to head back home. He had used the time to pick up the pasta, collect a newspaper, buy a scratchy that he knew would not produce any winnings, and indulge in a donut and a caramel thick shake from the kiosk in the centre of the mall. Andrew still treated food with reverence, savouring the richness and chewing slowly to make the flavour last, sipping his shake and relishing the cold sweetness that slid across his tongue. Lessons learned during his uneasy childhood would stay with him for many years to come.

He pushed his bike into the driveway, propping it against a verandah post, and waved to a neighbour trying to start his lawnmower. He turned the key in the door, listening for any sound. None came, and he strode up the hallway, fighting a sudden surge of unexpected fear that threatened to undermine his outward calm. He was relieved to see that the old man had not moved. He saw the open mouth with teeth yellowed by years of nicotine and stared at one bony leg twisted awkwardly beneath the other.

A walking stick was still hooked on the side of the chair that now lay on its back, the four legs surrounding the old man's head. Like the busker Andrew had seen once on a rare visit to the city, who balanced a chair stacked with pots and pans on his shoulders, dancing and playing the mouth organ all the while. Except his father lay still on the cold floor, and there was no music.

Andrew knew he had to phone the ambulance. He waited a few moments longer and dialled, checking for a pulse while he spoke and then following the instructions given over the phone. He remembered the neighbour and ran outside, signalling to the man over the deafening sound of the mower, leaving the door open and returning to his father's side. He knew it was too late, that the old man had gone, and he waited for some emotion to burst into his brain. There was nothing, no feelings of elation, of sadness or of guilt. His father was removed after police had examined the situation, taken photographs, and spoken to Andrew with sympathetic voices. They said he must have fallen after Andrew went down to the shops, slipping on his spilt beer and hitting his head on the table. The possibility of a heart attack was mentioned and they said he should have used his stick before attempting to stand, or at least waited until Andrew returned. The neighbour verified the time Andrew had left and the time he returned, telling the police that he was a good boy who looked after his father well, despite the old man's bad temper.

This time, there would be no guilt. Funeral arrangements and insurances kept him occupied for a while, with friends and neighbours calling by to offer their sympathy and help. For the first time in his life, Andrew was able to welcome them into his home, but the feeling was too new, too different for him to enjoy. He was glad when it was all over and the days gradually returned to normal. He turned the music up loud and cleaned away any evidence that his father had ever lived there, stuffing the bins with clothes and toiletries, magazines and old tools, beer cans and ashtrays.

Within weeks, he had rid the house of memories that prickled his skin and had started work on the yard. He called the council to pick up the old sofa from the back verandah and some of the timber from behind the shed. He parked his dad's Mitsubishi out the front with a for-sale sign across the windscreen and cleared the shed for his own use. Andrew had no intention of learning to drive, preferring to pedal or walk his way around town, and he decided to invest in a new racer with all the gear to match.

He continued his job at the supermarket, returning home after each shift and creating rich, imaginative meals for one. Andrew thought about getting a dog and searched online for one he could rescue, a kindred spirit that had suffered and endured as he had done since childhood. Something held him back, just as it did whenever he thought about finding his mother and brother. He had been alone for so long, even in the presence of others, that he did not know how to commit to the companionship of another being. He was afraid that he would be like his father.

As the winter set in, he burned the remaining yard wood in the smoky fireplace that had not been used for years and spent his evenings rugged up in front of the television. Weekends, he painted the rooms one by one and wandered around the empty house searching for a sense of satisfaction that eluded him. The days seemed so long, and the nights were spent in uneasy sleep. It wasn't what he had planned during the time his father was ageing and his own future held promise. He did what he had to do, but there seemed to be no pleasure in his newfound independence or the solitude that he had so often sought as a child.

Another year passed and Andrew spent more time on the computer than he did riding his bike. He researched Indigenous histories, chatted with friends that he had no intention of meeting up with, and read anecdotes from people living with abuse. The loneliness increased, and his life seemed pointless, empty, and going nowhere. He began to dread turning the key in the lock after work, opening the door to darkness, silence, and memories that resisted eradication.

Sometimes, he hoped for a knock on the front door, but when that night came he was unprepared, dropping his laptop and standing, hesitant, before edging his way down the hall. He could see the silhouette of someone through the opaque glass panel beside the entry, unrecognizable and perhaps even threatening. The figure repeated the knocking, waited, and then turned to leave. Andrew clicked the latch open, and the noise made the stranger spin around.

"Andrew? Are you Andrew?" The boy's voice was quiet, expectant, his face shadowy beneath the sensor light yet distantly familiar. But still Andrew was uncertain about answering.

"If you're Andrew, then I'm your brother. I'm Daniel. Danny. But you probably don't remember me. Sorry to shock you like this, but I've been looking for my family for months, since Mum died ..." His voice trailed off as he waited for Andrew to answer.

Andrew gripped the verandah rail at mention of the boy's mother, perhaps his mother.

"Mum died?"

"Last year. She gave me Dad's address when she was ill, but I lost it somewhere and have been trying to find the right Smith ever since. She said not to concern myself about father but to find her eldest son, my brother, and tell him she was sorry."

Andrew beckoned the stranger in, ushering him down the hallway into the kitchen that smelled of disinfectant and roasted vegetables. He offered Danny a soft drink and some chocolate cake that sat regally under a glass dome in the centre of the table.

"Did you make this?" Danny asked. "Mum used to make me chocolate cake, but I haven't had any since she died. Is Dad around?"

"Dad had an accident. Fell and hit his head on this table. I found him a couple of hours later, but he was gone."

Andrew waited for a response, but Danny just looked at him, his mouth full of cake. His eyes were dark like Andrew's, his black hair slicked upwards with gel, and his skin tanned as though he had been holidaying in Queensland. This was his brother, and Andrew was overwhelmed, feeling an urge to touch him, put his arms around the boy, and hug him tight. However, this was not a feeling he was accustomed to, so he just sat, not knowing how to react.

"We moved to the country," Daniel said between mouthfuls, "north of Brisbane where Mum got a job at a chicken farm. She worked there most of the time while I was growing up, but it eventually affected her lungs and she had to leave."

Questions filled Andrew's head, but he had difficulty in asking, not daring to believe that his brother had really returned and not wanting to face his mother's death. Instead, he blurted out a seemingly unrelated enquiry. "Did you get bullied at school like, you know, because you were black?"

Daniel finished his cake, laughing at the suggestion of racism. "Andrew, I lived in Queensland, for God's sake. Everybody was black at my school. Well, nearly everybody, and if anything, I got teased for being a whitey. It was all in fun though. Nothing serious, and my stepdad is pretty dark. I have a little brother and sister who are heaps blacker than you and me."

"I only had my dad, and I'm glad he's gone," Andrew said, looking directly into Daniel's eyes, not expecting a sympathetic response.

Daniel wiped his mouth before continuing. "Mum told me that he was no good, but even so, I wish I had known him. After all, I was just a little kid when we left. I still remember being hit though and having to eat all our dinner at the table while he watched TV. I remember you and how you protected me, taking the punishment without even crying."

"Oh, I cried all right," Andrew retorted, turning away from his brother's gaze. "I cried at night when Mum couldn't hear me." The memories saddened him, and he fidgeted with the dishcloth, wiping the chocolate crumbs into his hand and tipping them down the sink. "I don't want to talk about Dad anyhow. He was an evil man, and you are lucky you didn't know him."

The two young men chatted well into the night, Daniel willingly describing his family life to Andrew, who spoke more carefully, slowly, the bits and pieces of his childhood coming together in a tortured muddle of pain and unhappiness.

Daniel bunked on the couch that night, just as he would many times during the following months. There was so much life to catch up on, and Andrew realized that there had been rare moments of pleasure that sustained him through the difficult times. The friends who offered him their lunches, the brief concern of his principal, and the buns freely given by the delivery guys. Mostly though, he remembered those early-morning wanderings through the bush where the smells and sounds of plant and animal life overrode the stench of beer and cigarettes on his clothes.

Daniel found a job and accommodation in the city, investing in an old, panel van that he stored in Andrew's garage. On weekends, they loaded their bikes and headed to the country or the beaches that were a new experience for Andrew. Occasionally, they double-dated, meeting Daniel's friends in the city, visiting movie theatres, China Town, or just hanging out in the malls and city parks.

Stella was tall and lithe with a smile that showed the pink of her gums. Her red-brown hair and freckles attracted Andrew, while her love of the bush gave them something in common to talk about. Daniel was besotted with her sister Ingrid, and the two spent more and more time together as the months passed. Before that year was out, Daniel had decided to return to Queensland, taking Ingrid with him. He had mentioned the possibility to his brother many times, but that afternoon when Andrew returned home from work to find him loading the panel van with clothes and biking gear, the reality came as a shock.

"You're leaving then?"

"Yep. Told you I had to go eventually. You can tag along if you like. Meet up with your half-siblings." Daniel threw the last of his stuff in the back seat with the blankets and pillows from his flat. Stella and Ingrid came out of the house, their arms around each other and tears in their eyes.

"Stella is going to come up later," Danny said quietly. "So you can hitch a ride with her if today is too early to decide."

"Not planning to return then?" Andrew remained calm and outwardly cheery, but he felt the old anger rise and clenched his fist inside his pockets. His brother saw the emotion in those eyes that were so much like his own, but he never expected what happened next.

Without warning, Andrew grabbed Daniel by the shirtfront and shoved him against the car. "You come back into my life just to leave again. You can't do that, and now you are going to take my girlfriend too." His anger was brief and intense. He let go of Danny and pushed roughly past Stella, knocking her to the ground before racing up the steps into the house and locking the door.

"Shit. What just happened?" Daniel was astounded by his brother's outburst, and the way he had treated Stella seemed so out of character. Thinking about it later though, while driving the car that he had willingly shared with his brother on their weekend trips, Danny realized he should have recognised the signs much earlier. After all, his brother had grown up with the old man's bitterness and bullying. Something must have rubbed off and his mother had mentioned that, although she loved Andrew, sometimes he was just like his father.

Andrew stood inside the house with his back pressed to the door. He tried to control his rapidly beating heart with deep breaths, feeling increasingly angry with himself for venting unreasonable force on Stella and his brother. He heard the car start, the horn beep a final goodbye, and he sank to the floor. He was alone again, and a feeling of deep anxiety seeped throughout his body, making him visibly shake and hold his head with regret.

He closed his eyes and leaned his head back against the door as a sudden memory of his father's irrational rage surged through his mind. Except it was not his father; it was himself.

"The sins of the father," he whispered. The tears ran freely down his cheeks, and the darkness in the house deepened forever.

Old Jimmy

Old Jimmy was irate.

"They've taken my chair away. Replaced it with a palm tree, of all things."

Jimmy had been sitting on that chair, right near the front entrance, every week for close on thirty years. He liked to look out the window at the townsfolk walking past and to keep an eye on everyone who came into the pub.

"Not even a real one." Jimmy furrowed his brows and waved a flabby arm towards the offensive item. "It's made out of plastic. What's the point in having a plastic palm tree?"

His mates just nodded in agreement. They knew Jimmy would spend the rest of the evening complaining about the new managers bringing their modern ideas with them and rearranging the décor to suit a younger clientele.

"These new owners just don't care about their regular customers. Damned foreigners taking over the place, with their foreign food and foreign ideas."

Bazza, Nigel, and the other Friday-nighters just grinned and continued their conversation. It was easier to ignore the old guy's outbursts, even if they did side with him in this case. The renovations were not to their liking. Too modern for folk who had enjoyed the old ways as regulars, popping in for a drink after work or for a pie and chips while they watched the Saturday game. The bar was now in another section so that families could use the dining area. Nice move for newcomers, but they had not considered the longstanding patrons. Even the time-stressed furniture had been replaced by stainless steel and microfibre, while the heavy, wooden bar top, highly polished by many a greasy elbow over the years, had been chopped up and probably recycled as garden mulch or firewood.

Jimmy admitted the "foreigners" were all right really. Hard workers, with some Asian boss, and the food was good, the service impeccable. But he grumbled that it was not like the old times with a lot of the regulars moving on, replaced by partygoers and film buffs of indeterminate ages. The theatre was just across the railway bridge, and the young people filled in their pre-movie minutes by hanging around at the pub or the little diner next door. Gave old Jimmy plenty to complain about with their loud voices and foul language.

"And the girls are just as bad," he would say to no one in particular.

"He's in a time warp," the others would apologize to any bystanders. "Says the same thing day after day, and we are just waiting for the time when he cracks it and one of those young'uns retaliates."

Jimmy and his mates arrived regularly at the week's end for their evening meal and a play on the pokies, expecting and receiving special treatment from staff members who treated them as long-term friends. Age had reduced their numbers, but still some gathered and discussed the state of the town, the disrespect of young people, and the quality of the food that changed with each new chef. Occasionally, younger men would be invited to join the group, but they rarely lasted, unable to understand the entrenched opinions of the older guys who had seen the town grow from a few hundred to many thousand residents.

Jim came to this town close on thirty years ago, moved in from the farm when his wife got sick. They had no children, and they took time to adjust to living in such close proximity with the neighbours. After his wife died, Jimmy looked to the pub for companionship and a cheap meal.

He had been the oldest of ten children. Two brothers died in Vietnam, and he lost touch with his sisters as they married or moved interstate. Loneliness was a constant in his life, and he relied on his mates to keep the doldrums at bay. Sure, he had a younger brother who lived close by, but they hadn't spoken for years. Not since he married that black woman with all the kids and then went and added a few of his own. Baby Jimmy was the apple of his father's eye: plump, dark eyed and brown skinned, though paler than his stepsiblings and always laughing. He was named after his uncle Jim, although the two would never be close.

Old Jimmy insisted he was not related to Jimmy by the creek, even though they looked alike, except for the weight difference.

"Not by a long shot," he would comment irritably. "Nothing to do with me, and that woman was already pregnant when he married her. Could be anyone's kid."

He never saw the child, or the man he was to become. Often, sitting in his chair by the pub window, his grey eyes would follow a dark, young man down the street, and he would wonder if that was his brother's kid. But he never inquired. Small-town gossip travels fast, and he pretended not to listen when news of Jason's drowning and young Jimmy's depression was passed around the table.

Things changed the evening Bear walked in with another big guy in tow. The newcomer wore a black Akubra, which he politely removed, releasing a mop of tousled black hair. It matched the black shirt with the press-stud closures, and the boots that just needed silver spurs to complete the western look. He was tall and solid, with hands that spoke of outdoor work and a decent beard sprouting grey patches above his chin. He walked alone to the bar, leaving Bear to greet his friends. His reflection was stunted in the slanted mirrors that had replaced faded photos of local footy legends and cricket teams above the drinks cabinet but was still clear enough for him to see the stares and mouthed comments that his presence had inspired. It didn't matter to him, and even if he dressed more conservatively, there would still be the stares, especially in this town. Might as well dress the part and give them something to talk about, he would say to those who stood by him.

Old Jimmy saw Bear coming and frowned, turning his attention to the meagre seniors meal that barely filled his stomach. Never mind. He would get a pie on the way home and some chocolate biscuits to have with a coffee before bed. Bear stood quietly beside him.

"Hey, guys."

Never a talker, Bear waited for the conversation to start, noting the absence of yet another regular, but feeling neither curiosity nor concern for the absentee. That was the way he was, and someone would tell him in their own good time.

Old Jimmy crooked his head towards the newcomer. "Whatcha up to, Bear? Who's the other black bastard you got with yer?"

Bazza admonished the old guy, telling him to keep his language decent as not everyone could accept his brand of humour the way Bear did. Grey heads nodded in unison around the table, but all turned to get a closer look at the stranger in black.

"That's Sid. You know him. Tayo's cousin from up north."

"Cripes, so it is. That was a shock." Jimmy turned his attention back to the food, conversation over and the old feelings of betrayal and guilt returning. He had never forgiven Tayo for the deceit, just as he could never forgive his brother for marrying someone different. Bear was accepted because he hid nothing. People chuckled when Jimmy explained that Bear was one of the crowd, different but somehow the same, not denying his adoption or his colour.

"He's black as the ace of spades. How could he deny anything?" They laughed loudly but understood what Jimmy was trying to say and puzzled over their own mixed feelings. All those conversations they had in Tayo's presence, about racial taunts on the footy field, about the welfare payments Indigenous people received, and about saying sorry when nothing was their fault. Tayo had never said a word and let them believe he felt the same. They felt guilty because his unveiling threw things into an entirely different light. They had never really understood their own reasons for complaining. After all, Tayo was a good guy, one of their own for a time, yet he was one of the others.

Might seem trivial to outsiders, but this town is close knit, and although the folk might leave things be most of the time, there comes something like this and they react quietly, you know. They just avoided Tayo or talked behind his back, and eventually, he was so badly hurt and confused that he just couldn't cope. Most folk said it was a result of the accident and all those painkillers, but the rest of them knew it was his own guilt—he should have told them.

The accident messed with his brain and he just couldn't handle the criticism anymore. Went back with his cousin and did settle down a bit, leaving Sal to remortgage and pay off all the debts. One of his boys stayed, but he was too angry with his dad to be much help. The younger one moved to the city where he started to get into a lot of trouble. He's down in Barwon now, doing time for some robberies in the suburbs.

Tayo's cousin had returned to help Sal and decided he liked the place. He bought some property on the outskirts, just over the hill to the north of town. He could see the damage being done in the new estates and decided to plant his property down with trees and native grasses, creating land for wildlife. Council did not approve, but he persisted and eventually won his right because he was just far enough out of town. The neighbours respected his plans, and Sid began to mix with the locals, visiting the pub occasionally and learning how to tackle the hecklers.

Like Tayo, he had a good sense of business and allocated some of the acreage for housing. He had heard about old Jimmy's attitude and thought he would have a bit of fun, goading the old guy into an argument after Bear called him over to join the Friday nighters.

"Gonna bring the rellies down and settle them on my land. Got a permit to build seventy houses along the southern boundary. That's right about where your farm used to be, eh, Jimmy?" Sid grinned broadly, his white teeth emphasized in the subdued light of the dining area.

Old Jimmy didn't answer immediately, concentrating on his food and shovelling down the last few mouthfuls of Parmigiana. His mates waited, knowing there would be a reaction eventually, but even they didn't expect the old guy to explode so angrily. Jimmy slowly pushed his plate into the centre of the crowded table and looked up at the other guys, mumbling a few expletives before letting out his real thoughts.

"Pretty soon, we'll have the whole damned tribe here breeding snotty-nosed kids like rabbits, living it up with the alcohol, and leaving the area like a council dump." That was just the beginning. He flapped his flaccid arms at Sid, the sudden agitation causing him to send sprays of saliva across the table as he spoke, his ample chins wobbling in unison. His comments became louder, catching the attention of some young guys who had just walked through the door on their way to the bar. They had already been drinking, their attitude bordering on aggressive despite seemingly harmless shoves and camaraderie.

"Yeah! You got it, Pop. Tell 'em what you really think." They encouraged old Jimmy to continue the tirade, hooting and stomping their feet the angrier he became. Sid had stepped back from the table, surprised and concerned by the effect his jesting had on the old guy, and instantly worried that the gang would cause unnecessary trouble.

One young fella stood out as leader. He was tattooed heavily on both arms and his neck, with piercings in his nose and eyebrows, and was dressed in a light, sleeveless hoodie and coloured skinny jeans that revealed the wide elastic on his trunks. The rest of his group was attired in similar fashion, some with caps and sunglasses despite the evening dark. The boss man approached. He stood shoulder to shoulder with Sid and pushed his face close, his pointer finger stabbing against the black rodeo shirt that had caused so much attention.

"See how mad you've made the old guy? Have you no respect for your elders? We don't take too kindly to strangers in this town, especially those who pick on old guys like this. Time to move on, big fella." His lips curled against smoke-stained teeth, and his eyes creased into malicious slits as the others moved to support him.

Bear came up and stood behind his mate, quietly indicating that they should leave, but the interlopers barred their way. "Listen, guys." Bear commanded their attention. "There are families in here just enjoying a quiet meal. There are kids, and these old dudes are our friends. We have no beef with them, and you have to understand old Jimmy there didn't mean any harm. He's always like that. He'll get over it." Bear spoke quietly and slowly, adding that they could take the argument outside if necessary.

Bazza slid his phone from his pocket and held it beneath the table. He would call the cops if the matter escalated, although he had little doubt that Bear could mediate and calm the situation without fisticuffs. Like the others, he felt helpless and angry with himself for not being able to stand up in support of his mates like he had in his younger days.

And then it was over. Bear and Sid were known as passive blokes, but their size and demeanour were impressive, to say the least. The young guys must have thought better of it, and after a few cusses and gesticulations, they sidled out past the plastic palms and went elsewhere to look for trouble.

Bazza saw them later at the train station, and it dawned on him that they were end-of-the liners who had come from the western suburbs to sell their wares and have a bit of fun, returning home on the last train out before the cops found them. They were the strangers in town, not Sid.

In the meantime, Jim had calmed down and sat bewildered at the reaction to his tirade. Now he had to face his mates, and they could be pretty scathing when they thought anybody stepped too far over the line. He had been doing that a lot lately, going off his head with some stupid argument about foreigners and other intruders in his town. He thought about Bear and Sid, about his brother and the nephews he refuted. He thought about his age and how there was little left for him to enjoy and all the friends he had lost over the years.

He thought about Jimmy by the creek and how his illness prevented him from socializing or having a normal life. That was it. He knew what he had to do and decided this was the right time to contact his brother and perhaps finally meet with his namesake.

Old Jimmy struggled to get out of his chair. The weight on his legs seemed to glue him to the floor, and a shooting pain in his chest made him groan softly. He had trouble separating the dining room sounds from the words his mates were saying. Everything blurred in his head as he rocked into a standing position with Bazza and Nigel supporting him by the elbows. He felt an urgent need to find his family and shook off his helpers before heading tentatively out into the night.

Jimmy did have time to call his brother. He had kept the phone number pinned on his corkboard for the last few years, just in case he might need to call for some obscure reason. That night, it had taken Jimmy a long time to walk the short distance home, struggling to retain his balance and cope with increasing pain that threatened to destabilize his mind. He knew it was late but decided to call anyway, listening impatiently as the ring tones drilled into his brain, waiting to hear a voice that would span the lonely years and take him back to younger days. Someone picked up, and Jimmy sank to the floor, keeping the phone pressed tightly to his ear, whispering between those final, lucid moments of a fruitless life.

"It's me, Jimmy, your brother. I'm sorry ..."

A Stained Life

An old, stained-glass window stood rotting behind the shed, its colours hidden beneath eons of dust and fallen leaves. Nobody really knew, or cared, where it came from, but coincidentally, the dilapidated wooden church that stood at the eastern edge of town had one side window missing, the others crisscrossed with boards nailed to the greyed window frames. The church itself sat low amidst grassy knolls where thoughtless people had dumped their excess garden rubbish. The stumps that once held the building high above the damp undergrowth had long since rotted or sunk into the marshy ground, leaving the walls lopsided and the little front porch askew.

Now the shed on the town's northernmost perimeter, where the stray window stood, was being demolished as Ganan needed to clear the land before it was listed for sale. Still in his midtwenties, he had made a name for himself in the region as a hard worker and efficient businessman. Demolition and industrial cleaning kept his little team busy for most of the year, and he already owned his own house on a bit of land not far from the airport. Despite his ability to run a tidy and profitable business, the part he enjoyed most was the initial examination of each property, when treasures were unearthed and money could be made from recycling old building materials or metals.

The window was a find that appealed to his sense of history and artistic leanings. Carefully, he removed the timber and roofing iron that leaned against the window frame, scraped the mushy leaves from the glass, rubbed off some dirt with his sleeve, and gently lifted the relic out into the light. Remarkably, the glass sections were intact, although a few cracks in the lead joiners would need repair. The wooden frame, curved across the top part to accommodate a smaller, round window separated from the rest by a carved slat, had deteriorated badly and would probably require complete replacement. Ganan stood back to assess his find, seeing in his mind the processes he would follow to research and repair the jewelled colours and bleached wood in accordance with its origins. A ray of autumn sunshine flickered through the russet leaves of a maple planted by the homestead's founders over a hundred years past and glinted off the wiped glass triangles. The magic of this moment was not lost on Ganan, even though he was known for his practical rather than his sentimental nature.

Religion had no place in his life, although his mother had tried desperately to influence her son in the ways of her Catholic forebears. But churches, their structure and iconic decorations, their histories and spiritual aura, appealed to him. He knew of the old church and passed that way frequently during his working week. Self-sown trees had almost obscured the building from road users, but a gap in the foliage revealed the missing window. Someone had tacked an untidy square of chicken wire over the hole, possibly to keep out swallows and possums. Or youths in search of adventure.

Ganan decided to check the other windows remaining in the church just to ascertain that his find had come from there. With that purpose in mind, he left for work earlier than usual the next morning. He parked his truck on the neglected nature strip at the side of the building and walked down what was once a brick path that led parishioners to the arched front door. Dew dampened the trees and the unkempt grasses around the building, dripping coldly into his hair and soaking through his runners. He regretted leaving his boots in the car but only intended staying a few minutes. The windows were partly hidden by boards, but Ganan was able to take a few photos in the early light and planned to compare the designs he could see with his found window later that evening.

The old church stood on the front edge of a hectare of land that was now surrounded by future industrial sites and flat-roofed factories. Eventually, that land would be sold and cut up for more warehouses and depots where cheap imports would be assembled and delivered to local retailers or DIY enthusiasts building their new kitchens and garages. Somehow, it seemed wrong that this church, which had sustained the spiritual needs of the early settlers, had been so neglected and allowed to fall apart while businesses and shopping centres were constantly being updated to entice spenders into the town.

Ganan took his photos and headed back to the truck. As he sat in the driver's seat changing into dry socks and boots, he glanced back and saw a low mist forming beneath the trees and around the building. The night's dew had succumbed to the warmth in the early-morning sunrays slanting through the trees and formed an ethereal haze that swirled gently across the grass. It seemed to conceal the rubbish and broken boards, purifying the land and raising the church above human neglect. Ganan grabbed his camera off the seat and snapped a few more pictures, aware that he usually only took photos for the purpose of business or research.

But this was different. There was an aura about the church that intrigued him, and he determined to look further into its history and subsequent abandonment. He knew it had been Presbyterian and was one of the earliest buildings in town. He also knew that it was not mentioned in recent books written about the region. That fact excited him even more as it would be a challenge and also good publicity for his growing business if he could be the first to piece together some information that had previously been overlooked.

During his lunch break that same day, Ganan wrote a list of possible information sources with the historical society and the library at the top. There were church leaders he could speak to and his own mother had grown up in the town. She probably knew as much as anyone as her association with the church was pretty intense. He had already searched online, in the quiet hours of early morning, for at least a mention of the church building as well as the history of the land and the homestead where the window had resided for many years. There was nothing. It was as though it never really existed except as a relic in modern times. The more difficult the search seemed, the more intriguing it became.

Ganan loved this town. He had lived with his family right in the centre, close to the three churches and within walking distance of schools and train station, until the old house burned down after a lightning strike one hot summer. All his possessions had gone in an instance, and Ganan soon learned that he did not need that stuff around him anyway. He was content to live with the bare necessities, eventually furnishing his own house with sturdy recycled furniture and avoiding the acquisition of things that had no meaning.

Like his father before him, Ganan was built for physical work with a short, chunky physique, stumpy fingers always sporting a Band-Aid or two, and sandy-blond hair cropped close so the curls hugged his scalp tightly. His blue eyes and pale skin meant he had to protect himself from the harsh Australian sun, so high-viz shirts with long sleeves, sunglasses, and broad peak caps were his usual attire. He wore his heavy boots with long shorts nearly all year long, only changing to lighter socks and runners when the caked-on clay became uncomfortably heavy and the seasons dictated cooler garb. His father would have approved of his decision to restore the stained-glass find.

The window was stored in a dry workshop at the rear of Ganan's house, where he could begin the restoration. The photos proved it was identical to the ones remaining in the church, and it passed his mind that it should be returned to whoever now owned the old edifice. A better idea was forming in his mind. No one seemed to want the tumbledown structure or the land on which it had been built, and as far as he knew, there had never been any buyer interest recorded. If he could find the owners and convince them to sell, then returning the window might not be necessary.

That evening, Ganan took the photos of his artefact over to show Sylvi, his mother, bringing with him a couple of TV dinners and a slab of pear cider. He liked to check on her since his father had passed away the previous year, although he knew she was more than capable of looking after herself. Settled together on the comfy couch that had seen better days, mother and son looked over the photos he had transferred to her tablet and he listened to the old stories he had heard many times before on how the town had grown and how things had changed, not always for the better.

When Sylvi brought up the old church photos, she was silent for a moment and then told her son that he should stay away from that place. Bad vibes, she said, and it was better to let the old church rot into the ground, untouched and unattended.

"I want to buy it, Mum. It sits on a good piece of land and the church itself might be restorable. I'm off to the council tomorrow to get the name of the owner, and then I will decide where to go from there. You obviously know something about the old place, or you wouldn't be trying to put me off."

Sylvi looked at her son and knew it was no good trying to dissuade him. He had always been a determined young man, more so since his father had become ill. Ganan was still at school when he began working as a handyman, mowing lawns and clearing rubbish. For a while, his father would help him take any found metals to the recyclers, but once he got his driver's licence, Ganan worked alone. Eventually, he began employing his mates on a part-time basis until he had gathered a trustworthy team of hardworking young guys, some of who moved on to start their own demolition and cleaning businesses.

Gain 'n Loser, they called him, referring to the turnover of workers and joking about the way he made them slog long hours until each job was finished to his satisfaction. Often, he would be asked where his name originated, and most believed it was an invention of his parents.

"Depends which version of history you prefer," he would answer. "If you are Irish, it means 'white' or 'fair.' Got that from my dad's ancestors who migrated here along with other convicts. My mum's kin came from the outback, and the version I prefer means just that, 'from the west.' One day, I'll go out there and see if any of the family recognize me." Ganan laughed at his own joke, not revealing the fact that his relatives might be a whole lot blacker than he could ever be, despite his hard-earned, and rather meagre, tan.

A spate of new customers kept Ganan busy throughout that autumn and into the unusually dry winter months. Sudden rains at winter's end meant a welcome break from work, and he spent that time finishing the delicate restoration of the window frame. He enjoyed working with wood and had purchased new tools for the job, but only after asking the advice of a family friend and local artisan specializing in stained glass and its framework.

Uncle Ned, as Ganan knew him, recognized the window and was at first hesitant, wondering if it had been stolen. He was also cautious because he had heard the stories, told behind closed doors, about incidents that involved the church elders and some local children, many years ago. For him, the ghosts of the past still existed, and he cautioned Ganan about purchasing the tainted land.

"What is it with this place, that no one wants to tell me the details? No matter where I look or whom I ask, people just say to stay away, not get involved, because there are things you don't want to know. Well, I do want to know, and I will eventually find out what happened to make everyone so secretive." Ganan was getting a little impatient as the months went by and still no one was willing to come forward to discuss the possibility of selling the apparently undesirable land. He had written several times to an agent for the owners, his name supplied by the local council, but had received no acknowledgement. Perhaps they thought that if they ignored him he would go away, just as his mother and the other townsfolk avoided his questioning in the hope that he would eventually lose interest.

Apparently, the original church elders had decided to rid themselves of the property after people stopped attending, during the years of the Great Depression. It was not poverty that drove the townsfolk away but a falling out with a particularly opinionated minister. Uncle Ned remembered his own father telling him about the minister whose influence made him turn away from organized religion to become a nonbeliever.

"Not an atheist," Ned explained, shaking his grey head and using his hands to emphasize this point. "My father still believed in some kind of spiritual association with his forbears and told us that his family had been coerced into the Christian religion." Ned again shook his head, telling Ganan that it was not bad to join the church, but people should be allowed to keep their own spiritual beliefs without fear of going to hell.

Ned was supposedly his mother's cousin and Ganan had admired his craftsmanship since he was a child. The studio and workshop that sat covered in espaliered fruit trees and grape vines down the back of Ned's bluestone cottage had been a source of inspiration for the awestruck boy. He had spent many hours watching Uncle pedalling the vintage lathe, carving beautiful bowls, chair legs, and intricate candlesticks from recycled timber or pieces of wood found in the shrinking bush lands around town. Most of all, he was fascinated by the collection of Aboriginal artefacts that lined the studio walls interspersed with Ned's own dot paintings and decorated boomerangs.

Ned would watch the boy standing back, his eyes searching the creations and avoided answering his questions about the meanings hidden in the artworks. "You look like your dad," he would often say. "But you think like your mum, although she has mellowed in recent years. Just appreciate what you can see, and don't try to complicate life by looking too deeply. They are just pictures." After all, Ned had been born in the town and knew little about his Indigenous heritage. The paintings were personal, and he felt he had no right to claim that the stories they told were traditional. They had come only from his imagination, from somewhere deep in his soul.

Ganan took his advice and simplified his living even more as he grew into a man. However, there were questions that stirred his imagination and sometimes he could not let go, digging deeply into histories that roused his curiosity. The old church and its surrounding paddocks were one item he could not easily put aside.

"You are like a little puppy with a soft toy, Ganan," his mother said affectionately. "Once you get an idea in your head, you worry it to death, shaking out all the stuffing that makes it what it is and taking the pieces apart, never to be returned to their original state. You open up old mysteries and your life changes. Everybody's life changes."

"All I ask is that you lead me in the right direction. If you can't, or won't, tell me the story about this window, then at least tell me who can."

"Ganan, I only know what I have been told, and that isn't much. There was some Reverend James, or Jones or something, that punished the children in his congregation quite regularly. Apparently, he brought in some kids from up around the Murray who had mixed blood. Ned's dad was one of those boys. They were supposedly fostered by the reverend and his wife, but they were treated badly and made to conform to his standards. Something went on in that church that I don't even want to think about, and this guy, together with one or two of his mates, used those children for their own pleasure. Remember that was many years ago, long before the Depression, and attitudes were very different from today."

"Not so different, Mum. Don't you read the news about paedophile rings and slavery of children? Even now, there are people who can't speak about things that have happened to them because it is too traumatic, or they feel they will be accused of lying."

"Yes, but that doesn't happen here. Not in this town," Sylvi said with just a hint of cynicism in her words. "People would not allow it to happen if they knew. That particular minister made sure those little boys kept quiet and the rumours were always quashed. That was a time when people did not speak of such things and probably would have blamed the children anyway, especially since they were black. All of them are gone now, but even as old men, they said nothing, so this is just hearsay."

"But someone must have found out because the church closed down." Ganan tried to put the pieces together in his mind and still could not understand what his stained-glass window had to do with that grey past.

"Maybe you'd better speak to your uncle Ned, although I don't think he knows much more than I do." Sylvi busied herself with the dishes, wiping away the crumbs from their conversation and letting her son know that she did not want to discuss the matter further.

Ganan did eventually speak to his uncle Ned, knowing that he might not learn anything new. Ned was much older than cousin Sylvi and had seen the town grow from isolated farmhouses and hills covered with straggly sugar gums and tussock grasses into a thriving railway town. He had watched the freight trains bring wheat and barley in from the northern regions and remembered the corrugated iron sheds beside the tracks, where the grain was stored and pigeons flocked in their hundreds. Now he lived surrounded by new-century supermarkets and sporting stadiums. He missed the simplicity of his old life but understood that progress brought a wealth he had certainly benefited from, as clients moved into the town's growing shopping malls and estates.

Ned's expertise and reputation had grown alongside the town's expansion and extended to the city where his work can be seen in high-rise offices and hotel foyers. His paintings had become popular with new homebuyers because he refused to charge exorbitant prices for something he took pleasure in creating. However, his stained-glass creations and restorations, especially those depicting Indigenous legends, raked in the money, setting him up for a comfortable retirement in his self-built cottage.

Ganan had packed the window carefully in bubble wrap and loaded it into the back of his truck, strapping it down under blankets and an old tarpaulin. Uncle Ned helped him unload, and they carried it into the studio for the old man's appraisal. He was very impressed with the restoration work but cautioned Ganan about prying too deeply into the church affair.

Running his fingers over the polished glass sections, Ned spoke quietly, as though he was talking to himself, not his young visitor. "You know my own father helped build that church, when he was just a boy. He told me about the windows and how the sun shone through to make rainbows on the old wooden floor."

He turned to Ganan and explained a difficult part of his life from when he was much younger. "Your mum and I aren't really cousins, you know. Her family is from a mob in West Australia. They came here during the fifties and I became friends with her older brothers. She was born here though, and we called ourselves cousins because it was easier than explaining. Anyway, people said we all looked the same, so we just left it at that."

"Yeah. I understand. I don't bother explaining why I am white and my mother has dark skin. No point really. You came down from the Murray River somewhere, didn't you, Uncle Ned?"

"Not me, but my dad was brought here when he was just a little tyke. The local church took him in, and he lived in a shed out the back of the reverend's house, with a couple of other kids, next door to the church"

Ned pulled up a chair and sat close to the stained-glass window, occasionally reaching out his hand to feel the new wood and the dimpled glass triangles. "My dad helped make this window, you know. When he was just a teenager."

Ned repeated this snippet of information about his father's building prowess. "That shed you demolished at the old homestead, where you found the window, that was my dad's workshop for a time. That was after he married my mother."

Ganan drew in a deep breath and expelled it with a sigh. "Why didn't I know this before?" he questioned his uncle, a slight irritation in his voice and his eyes wide with surprise. "Is that where you learned your craft? Was he one of the reasons the church closed down? Do you know why the window was out?"

So many queries filled his head all of a sudden, and he wanted answers immediately. Ned knew very little about his father's upbringing and struggled to remember the few things he had heard through small-town gossip.

"'Silence is golden' was his motto. My dad had problems being with other people, and whenever my mother invited friends or relatives over for dinner, he would disappear down the back paddock. I remember him coming home after dark and sneaking into the house to avoid any confrontation with my mum. Their relationship was difficult, and he definitely had social issues."

"Do you think he might have been abused by someone in the church? Perhaps the minister who took him in and supposedly cared for him?"

"Don't really know. He never volunteered much information about his childhood. But of the four boys who were brought down from the river country, two of them took their own lives in later years and the other one ended up being locked away with some kind of mental issue. It was like Dad had lost his brothers. Apart from his silence, he was OK most of the time. He had his woodwork to keep him occupied, and he had a tidy little business restoring and making distinctive, carved furniture. I do know he hated the church."

"But that doesn't explain why the building has been abandoned for so long." Ganan had not finished with the questions and wanted to know more about the window.

"Don't push it, boy. You might get more than you bargained. I don't know the whole story, but there is something in that building that is not quite right."

"What do you mean, Uncle Ned? Are there bodies or something? Who removed the window, and why?"

"Listen, Ganan. There is an old fellow down at the historical society who apparently knew the boys, in their later years, of course. He might be able to help because I know very little, and I don't know which parts of the story are true or what has been fabricated."

Ned scribbled a name on a yellow sticky, handing it to Ganan across the window that was propped on a short-legged metal easel. Light from the open door made the reds and greens of the glass glow with surreal colour, while the darker blacks and blues remained strangely ordinary.

Leaving the window in the care of his uncle, Ned headed for home, happy that he had at least found out a little about the people involved in the mystery. He wanted the building and land more than ever now and was determined to contact the owners, no matter where they were hiding.

It was several days before Ganan had time to pursue his window mystery. Work was full on at that time of the year as customers took advantage of the warmer spring days and tidied their homes for the upcoming festive season. There were new pergolas to be built and old fences to be replaced, sheds erected to cater for summer barbecue parties or to store useless overflow from the chockfull homes. Ganan could never understand why people required so many things to clutter and complicate their lives. He was content in his minimalist environment, or at least he was until he found the window.

The yellow note remained on his desk for a while until he decided to telephone, his curiosity deepening every time he drove past the old church. A time was arranged one afternoon for him to speak with the amateur historian.

Stuart had lived in the region for all of his seventy-something years and knew more about its history than anyone. His home was a veritable museum. Walls were hung with prints and paintings of the area while desktops, benches, and chairs were stacked with books or paperwork that he was working on at that time. Ganan doubted that they ever moved, noting the cobwebs and dust on several stacks. He shook his head in disbelief at the amount of paraphernalia Stuart had amassed in the name of research. There seemed to be no method in storing the collections, but each time Ganan touched on a particular subject, Stuart knew exactly where that information could be found.

"Now, at this stage I don't know much about the church itself or the reasons for its closure, but I do know that Ned's old father was determined not to let anyone back into the place. He didn't offer any reasons, never spoke much anyway, but just said there were memories in there that no one should be burdened with."

Stuart beckoned Ganan through his lounge room where a narrow pathway wound between piles of books and boxes, shelves of old radios and bottles turned purple with age. He explained that they were in storage, ready to be packed up and displayed in the local museum when it was finally extended.

"We've been trying to get this extension built for ten years now, and in the meantime, my house is used to collate and store all this stuff. Don't worry. I'm not a hoarder in the sense of the word, and not many of these things actually belong to me."

A sudden idea popped into Ganan's head, and he thought he might find a way of getting the locals to voice their opinions on the sale of the church or at least pressure the owners to sell.

"Stu, the old church could be restored and used as a museum. If I could buy the land, I might be able to lease the building back to the community. I am sure there are people here who would like to see a bit of history resurrected."

"Perhaps. Maybe the new residents, but there would certainly be opposition from those who know what went on and who believe in letting ghosts sleep."

"I tried the front door, but it seems to be locked. Do you reckon anyone would complain if I just climbed through the missing window and had a look?"

"I guess you could try, but don't expect me to stand up for you when you're caught. Probably better to get permission from the owners first."

"Can't find them. I've written heaps of letters and tried to make phone calls, but they just don't answer. I don't even know if I am writing to the correct people."

Later that day, Ganan phoned one of his workers and prepped him on a break-in. Jordy was astounded that his painfully honest boss could even consider something illegal, and he jumped at the chance to be a part of what he called "an expedition into the unknown."

The following evening, when a sliver of moon was rising in the east and the retiring sun glowed orange behind the twin hills west of the town, the two young men unloaded a ladder from the truck, donned their work gear, and walked casually down the side path of the church. Just two repairmen checking the safety of the old building or perhaps removing some trapped wildlife from inside. Either way, they had their excuses ready in case someone questioned their intentions.

Jordy folded back a corner of the chicken wire and climbed through the window, dropping silently onto a wooden bench that sat conveniently against the wall. He checked the front door and called to Ganan that it was locked, strangely, from the inside with a heavy padlock. Ganan passed a smaller ladder through the window to make their exit easier and joined his accomplice in the musty dark of the church, using his work torch for light.

Curtains of cobwebs draped across the high ceiling beams and dribbled down to the floor. A few roofing shingles had broken and lay on the dais. Leaves had fallen through the cracks and spread across the first rows of seats, rustling gently with the movement of the intruders. All the furniture seemed to be intact, and several paintings, their subjects obscured by dust, hung crookedly on the timber-lined walls.

Heavy, oak pews remained where they had been left at the front near the pulpit, while wooden benches for the poorer people stood in uneven rows towards the back of the church. A small, doorless room, possibly for children attending Sunday school, opened on one side, and a closed lean-to could be seen on the right. From the outside, this odd addition was the only section of the building that had not sagged out of shape, its stumps and walls still solid after so many years.

"What are we looking for?" Jordy whispered in the eerie enclosure, his torch searching dust-filled corners and attracting velvety moths into the moving light beams. A circle of cockroaches, feasting on a tiny, dead bat, scuttled away as a loose floorboard creaked underfoot.

"Just something to explain why this place is taboo. Whatever you can find, I guess." Ganan ran his gloved hand across the pulpit, releasing clouds of dust that made him sneeze. A purple, velvet curtain had been tacked beneath the top, its threads now thin and torn with age, the folds and creases heavy with layers of grime. At Ganan's touch, the material suddenly succumbed to time and the weight of the dirt, ripping from the tacks that held it in place. It lay in a dusty heap on the dais, releasing shiny, black house spiders that crawled hastily back beneath the safety of the folds.

Startled, Ganan moved back a step and shone his torch on the thick, central spine that supported the sloping top boards. Words scratched into the oak upright caught his eye, and he bent to take a closer look. "They won't look here" was etched in a childish hand and barely decipherable. Ganan thought that maybe it was a hiding place for children playing games, where they would be invisible beneath the purple shroud and protected by the holy location.

"Hey, look at this, Jordy," he called between sneezes, vigorously rubbing eyes that were becoming increasingly irritated in the musty air. "Looks like the words have been scratched in with a pocketknife or something. I wonder who they were hiding from and when they were written."

Jordy examined the post and ran his hand over the shallow carvings, intrigued by words that must have meant something to the reader all those years ago.

"Maybe it was the little foster kids that scrawled this stuff into the wood when the minister wasn't looking. Maybe this is where they hid when they got into trouble. It would have easily hidden two kids between the curtain and the back board, just behind that middle support."

Jordy shone his torch across the littered floor in the direction of the lean-to. "Should we check out that little room? Looks as though it was constructed at a later date than the original building. Maybe for storage or something."

A padlock prevented them from entering, but the surrounding wood had rotted enough to shove the door inwards, splintering the jamb into shards that crackled underfoot. Where the main hall had some natural light seeping through the stained-glass windows, the peculiar space behind the broken door was completely dark. A sour smell pervaded the room and caused the two intruders to step back, pulling their shirts up over their noses.

"Gawd, what's that stink?" Jordy's voice was muffled beneath the protective material, which did little to filter the stench. "I could smell it from outside, but I only thought it was from that pile of dumped rubbish. This is disgusting. I'm not going in there!"

Ganan moved into the doorway while shining his torch across the floor and up the walls. He hesitated moving into the low-ceilinged room that was not much bigger than a kitchen pantry, but his curiosity got the better of him. He stepped down a level onto a thick layer of organic matter. A narrow gap between the step and the main building revealed the origin of the stench. It seemed a possum had recently managed to enter the room but got stuck on the way out and died in situ, its fluffy tail and hindquarters jammed tightly where its struggling had displaced a skirting board.

The smell was too strong, and Ganan hastily retreated. As he turned to have a final look, his torch beam landed on something hanging off the wall to the right of the unfortunate creature. Two metal rings with chains attached, their links partly covered by accumulated debris, aroused his curiosity, but the foul air prevented a closer examination, and Ganan decided to go back at a later date.

The trespassers had seen enough for one day, although they were disappointed that they had found no tangible reason for community negativity surrounding the church. Ganan stood outside at the top of the ladder and started to pull the smaller ladder back through the window when he noticed a movement near the broken lean-to door. He swept his torchlight across the area and caught a flash of something he could not explain, but it disappeared too quickly for him to focus the light on any particular spot.

"Probably a possum dropped through the broken shingles." Jordy shuddered as an unexpected cool breeze cut through the warm night air. "Let's get out of here and come back during the day. I don't think anybody is going to care if we break in again to remove the dead animal. Then we can have a proper look around."

It was not until later that night that Ganan recalled the iron rings and tried to imagine their purpose. He lay awake going over the night's events, the writing under the pulpit, the spiders and insects that inhabited the old building, and the smell of rotting flesh. There had been a sense that they were not alone in the church, and Jordy too had felt uneasy, as though they were being watched. And then that sudden movement as they climbed back through the window worried Ganan. He was too practical to believe in the spirit world but felt an inexplicable sense that the past was invading his present.

Next morning, Stuart called by. He had been sorting through some old books and discovered a short letter addressed to "My Friend, from Keenan."

"Keenan was the guy who had been locked in a mental institution for most of his adult life. He was one of the river country children brought down to this town and raised by the reverend. There are some things you should read, although it makes no sense to me."

Ganan took the letter, noting the methodical and precise spacing of words on the lined paper.

"I think Keenan was one of the previous owners mentioned in the information I got from the council. Keenan and Tom Smith. It was the agent I had to contact though."

There had been a date on the letter at one stage, but it was faded and unreadable, as were some of the sentences. He eagerly inspected the parts that were available, searching for some clue as to why the window had been removed and why the townsfolk had never bothered to reopen the old church.

"Dear Friend," the letter opened, "I told you they would never look under the curtain, but I was wrong and am very sorry for getting you into trouble. Thank you for not telling them that I carved those words into the pulpit. We were just children, but I will never forget how you protected the three of us."

Ganan explained the discovery of the etched words to Stu and told him about the door being padlocked from the inside and how the window had been pushed outwards when it had been removed. Certainly not a job for one man even though the window was fairly small. There must have been at least two people involved in the removal.

The letter continued with words sometimes so faded that Ganan had to fill in the spaces.

"When I am gone, you must go back into the church and burn it down. If that is too difficult, then you should lock the doors from the inside so no one can enter. The window must be removed. Do you remember that the light always shone through the glass, making Reverend Jones look divine, and he said that was why we had to obey his wishes? Because that was God's light shining on him. But he was less than holy, an evil man, and that window ..."

The words, penned so eloquently, disappeared midsentence, and Ganan was again left with unsatisfactory answers.

"This must have been written to Ned's father, Tommy, or one of the others. It seems to be from an adult and done after the church became redundant. One thing is for sure: they were definitely well-educated, even though they supposedly suffered some cruelty at the minister's hands." Ganan thought deeply for a minute, repeating the names quietly to himself. "Keenan and Tom. Owners of the land. Was it passed on to Ned?"

He carefully folded the letter and replaced it back inside the book where Stuart had discovered it. "You know something, Stu? I think Ned and my mum know more than they say, and I am going to get to the bottom of this church thing."

Stuart looked at him and knew that Ganan was stubborn enough to continue searching as long as questions remained. He stopped the young man from leaving, grabbing his sleeve and closing the door. "I know who owns the land."

Ganan stood silent for a moment, surprised and offended that someone had kept that information from him for so many weeks, perhaps even months.

"Before you get angry, I did not know about the ownership until last night. You see, there was something else with the letter. A title deed and detailed explanations that placed ownership with the four men who had been transported here as kids. Apparently, they bought the church and land in later years, after people stopped attending and Reverend Jones left town. How they raised the money we will probably never know, but it has a covenant preventing any future sale until two generations have passed. Ned and his brothers were the immediate beneficiaries, but they probably knew very little about the will and title deed. Now there is only Ned and his kids. I don't think he knows anything about the land either, and even if he did, he has a great respect for his deceased elders and would probably do nothing anyway. I guess you will have to wait to buy the place. At least until Ned has gone."

"That's why my letters and phone calls to the property managers went unanswered. They have been put into someone's 'too hard' box and forgotten. We have the deed, but surely someone paid rates all those years, or did they get an exemption because it was church land?"

"I don't know the story with that matter, but there is something else. After Mrs. Jones died, supposedly from injuries received in a fall, the minister just disappeared. He had earned the disrespect of many in the town, so they just said, 'Good riddance,' and left it at that. However, there were rumours that he had been murdered and buried on church property. Just rumours, you understand."

Ganan could see that Stuart was increasingly uncomfortable with the conversation and decided to leave. He had other ways of solving this problem, and he might even enlist the services of a property lawyer.

"Stu, this is all too complicated and difficult. I think I will take your advice and leave it alone, at least for a while. Maybe a few years down the track I might look into it again, and in the meantime, you can keep that title deed hidden and Ned can look after the old window."

"Good lad, Ganan." Relieved, Stuart closed the door after his visitor left and sat quietly amongst his collections. However, the abruptness of Ganan's decision puzzled him, and while he wanted to believe that the matter could be put aside, he decided that Ned and Sylvi should be informed on the latest developments.

In the meantime, with his own curiosity well and truly awakened, he would do a little more private research.

Ned's Legacy

Sylvi picked up the phone, annoyed that anyone would call so early in the morning.

"Ned. What on earth do you want at this hour? What's happened?"

"No, nothing. I am just concerned that Stu is doing some pretty intense hunting and will eventually uncover the truth. We might have to tell Ganan the whole story, as we know it, so that he understands why our hands are tied."

"You woke me up for that?" Wrapped in her favourite purple dressing gown, Sylvi rested the phone on her shoulder and wandered around the house while picking up clothes, newspapers, and last night's supper dishes.

"Sylvi, you know it's important. If this gets out, there will be no end of questioning, and I am too old to be involved in any controversy."

"You are already involved." Sylvi laughed. "Did you really think it would just go away? Anyway, your kids could benefit from the sale of the land. Maybe your dad should've burnt the building down all those years ago, and then there would've been nothing to worry about."

"I don't think bones burn, Sylvi. They might crumble a bit, but they would still be there for all the world to see."

Sylvi switched on the old kettle, speaking loudly over the noise. "Look, Ned, if you are really concerned, then I will ask Ganan to stop by after work, and we will have a chat. You can try to explain the -- the subterfuge."

"That's a bit harsh, Sylvi. Not a word I would use. Maybe deceit, but not subterfuge."

"How about *lies?* I will tell Ganan about our lies."

Ned disapproved of his cousin's bluntness, and the irritation showed in his voice. "Just call him, Sylvi, before he contacts some legal people."

It was early afternoon before Sylvi remembered to call her son, and arrangements were made to discuss the events of the past year regarding the dilapidated old church. Ganan always looked forward to an evening meal with his mother, even though he usually supplied the food and drinks. This time, he had some news of his own to tell her.

He left the job early, showered, and put on clean work clothes. Ganan believed in economizing with the washing and reckoned his mum would not mind if he wore his high-viz shirt to dinner. That way, he could sleep in it and get up for work next morning almost dressed. He drove past the old church on the way to his mother's new house, calculating in his head the time and money he would need to spend on stabilization and renovation. One way or another, he would buy the property that hid so many secrets.

"I went back to the church, Mum." Ganan spoke as soon as he walked through the heavy oak door. "Used bolt cutters and broke the padlock from the inside. Now anyone can get in through the front door, but don't worry. We closed it again so it still looks locked."

"Dammit, Ganan. You don't know what you have done." Sylvi was obviously upset by her son's actions. "Now there will be trouble."

Ganan had expected that kind of reaction and continued as though he had not heard the concern in his mother's voice. "We removed the dead possum. Put it in a plastic bag and sprayed some disinfectant all around so we could have a closer look at that little room. While we were unplugging lumps of fur from the boards, we noticed something else." He waited a moment, testing the effect of his words, watching Sylvi's dark eyes for a response.

"Bones. We found finger bones under the floorboard. And black material that fell apart when we touched it, but we didn't go any further. After all your secrecy and refusal to give any details, we kind of expected a body, but when it actually became real, it was pretty much a shock to the system."

The sound of breath drawn through clenched teeth made Ganan turn suddenly. His skin prickled as an unnatural and momentary sense of the spirit world flashed through his mind then just as quickly disappeared when he saw Uncle Ned striding into the kitchen.

"I told you to let old ghosts lie, Ganan. You had no right to disturb that ground, and you don't realize what repercussions we will all have to deal with if this gets out." Ned's voice was unsteady, his face red with controlled rage as he fronted up to the young man.

"No need for it to get out, Ned." Stuart shuffled bandy-legged through the front door without knocking. "I have lain awake all night just thinking about this problem, and I can see a way to let sleeping dogs lie and satisfy all our needs. Ganan can purchase the land, I can inspect the building and give approval for renovation, we can turn it into a museum, and nobody need know what lies beneath the original floor." Stuart knew he wouldn't be around to face any implications, and he had no family reputation to worry about.

Sylvi sighed with relief, as Stuart sounded so positive. She asked Ganan to call Jordy in, as they could not afford to have loose ends that might be their undoing. He needed to know the story just as much as Ganan, and the little group had to have confidence in his ability to keep secrets.

"What do you mean, Stuart? How can you give approval?" Ganan's usual curiosity took precedence over any polite greetings, and questions filled his thoughts.

"And hello to you too, Ganan." Stuart grinned and ran long, bony fingers through his untidy mop of grey hair. "I was a structural engineer and occasionally do building inspections in my very limited spare time. I'm pretty keen to keep the building as a museum for all my collected data. I also understand and respect Ned's need to honour his father's wishes and to avoid family or legal complications."

"Mind you," Sylvi interrupted, "I would not be at all surprised if there are others in this town who know the full story. The oldies around here don't like to rock the boat. They tend to keep things to themselves and avoid gossip." Then she added thoughtfully, "I wonder how many other secrets have gone to the grave with their keepers."

"The lean-to is intact." Ganan's mind raced as he absorbed these new revelations and possibilities. "We could just put new flooring over the top of the old stuff and pretend ignorance as to what is underneath. It's a small area with no need for plumbing or power, just for storage, like a garden shed or something." His enthusiasm showed, and Stuart joined in, picturing shelves of historical artefacts and paperwork lining the rough-hewn walls.

"Nobody need know. If something happens in the future after we have passed on and the bones are disgorged by floods or fire, then Ganan and Jordy can claim innocence, blame it on us, and nobody will be the wiser."

Ned laughed, remembering how his father had always told him just to shut up and take what comes. "Blame it on the blackfellas, you mean, Stu. That's OK. My dad had broad shoulders and never baulked at taking the blame. He said it was easier than trying to prove innocence."

Sylvi disappeared into the kitchen, still worried that her son would eventually be the one who had to face complications in the future and to live with the secret in the immediate present. However, it did seem to be the most practical solution, sweeping the rumours under the rug, or at least under the floorboards. She chuckled at her own private joke and loaded a tray with chips, nuts, and pear cider. This was going to be a long night of conversation where all the bumps and unknowns had to be ironed out smoothly.

Ganan's practical nature made him question the necessity of silence. "I don't really understand all the fuss, especially if this thing happened so many years ago. It doesn't actually involve any of us, does it?" He could not fathom the family's need to keep things quiet, or their overwhelming desire to respect the wishes of the dead.

Ned pulled up a chair and sat quietly for a moment, his gnarled hands clasped and his downturned face hidden beneath long, grey locks and wiry beard. He beckoned Ganan and the others to sit down so he could relate the whole story, or at least as much as he knew. Much of it was guesswork that he had pieced together from memories of conversations with his father and from Stuart's acquired knowledge. Sylvi too had contributed, although her understanding had been gained in recent years.

"This is my legacy, but it affects us all and I am just not willing to publicly unearth all this subterfuge." Ned looked sideways at Sylvi, but she had not noticed his reference to their phone conversation earlier in the day. "You know my father was a very private man, so everything I know about him has just been picked up in bits and pieces over the years. I will tell it as I know it."

Ned had spent the previous night going over his father's life, organizing his memories and writing it all down as best he could. Copies were made, and he handed them out to the others, apologizing for probable grammar and spelling mistakes. The information all fitted on a couple of pages and read without breathing space. After all, Ned was an artisan, not an academic.

He read sections of his own notes out loud, emphasizing some points of interest and adding to others. Soft Irish music played in the background, and it occurred to Ganan that this was entirely inappropriate for such a narrative, but he kept his mouth shut both for his mother's sake and for memories of his father.

Ned's voice was low as he read, his listeners deeply involved in the tale, their eyes on the paper and their sympathies fixed on stolen lives.

"Tommy was taken from his mother back in the 1920s." Ned hesitated momentarily before continuing.

> They had lived on the Murray River, Millewah he called it, and he was the bastard child of one of the station owners up that way. Four kids were taken, two of them quite white and the much darker Keenan and Tommy. The boys never went back to find their families because they thought they would be rejected. There are school photos from that time, taken here in this town, that show the boys hidden away at the back, even though they were apparently quite small and should have been at the front. Reverend Jones took them in and put beds out in the shed behind his house, *The Manse*, which was not far from the church. They ate and bathed in the house under the supervision of Mrs. Jones, who died fairly young from injuries

she received in an accident. Tommy said she was always having accidents and was afraid of Mr. Jones. They had to work hard cleaning the church and keeping the gardens tidy. Sometimes, if Jonesy was angry, they would hide under the pulpit in the church because they believed God would protect them there and if they sat very still, no one would find them. Keenan was a good writer and would often leave messages on the wooden underside of the pulpit. He used charcoal to write, or his pocketknife. The boys also learned how to repair furniture, and they helped renovate the old church, probably when they were about ten years old. They learned how to cut the glass for the windows and were punished if they were clumsy and wasted the precious materials. I remember the scars on my father's arms from the broken glass. Mr. Jones had friends who would come into the shed at night, and Tommy would never tell me what happened there but he said the two whiter boys were the favourites and were sometimes given treats as a reward. Tommy and Keenan would be punished because they refused to co-operate and were tied in the lean-to, chained to some rings on the wall overnight. Left without food and water, or blankets, threatened if they made a sound, then taken back to the shed in the morning before anyone needed to use the church. They were told the Devil would come in the night and take them if they cried out. Some of the parishioners must have got wind of what went on because many people stopped coming, and Tommy said they went to the Methodist church closer to the town centre. Mr. Jones used the window to intimidate the boys, pointing out that the sun shone through the coloured glass and glowed on him while he gave his sermon. That made him holy and he had to be obeyed. They were just kids. They believed him.

When the parishioners left, Mr Jones became more violent and his wife died. The boys were teenagers by then and no longer living in the shed. They went to work in the town and Tommy became a furniture maker or carpenter. None of them were very happy boys, but they saved their money, and when the church land came up for sale a few years later, they got together and bought it. Reverend Jones still lived at *The Manse* and seemed to have some control over the boys, even though he was no longer working as a minister and had gone a bit weird. One day, they found him inside the church with another boy, and Keenan lost it. He was a big man at that stage and strong from working on the dairy farm on the other side of town. He was raging and gave Jonesy an almighty punch right in the face. The little kid disappeared pretty quick and no one knows who he was. Probably long gone now, but he might have told what happened. Jonesy fell into the lean-to and never came out. The guys buried him beneath the floorboards, and that's where he remains today.

Both of the lighter skinned boys who had provided pleasure for Mr Jones and his cronies took their own lives eventually, and their claim on the land passed to Tommy and Keenan, who had trouble living with their actions and with the guilt from their childhood. Keenan died many years ago in a mental institution, from a skin disease that the doctors said was psychologically induced. Stress related. Tommy kept his promise not to pass the property on to anyone else, and I inherited it on condition that it would never be sold while either myself or my children were alive. My kids don't know I own the property. If they did, they would try to make me sell up because they have no respect for their ancestors. Sylvi knows the story because she helped nurse my dad when he

> was dying. His mind wandered a bit at that stage, and he occasionally relived his childhood traumas. Mostly though, he was silent. We kept his secrets and made sure no one could enter the church. My dad had padlocked the door on the inside and removed the offending window, replacing it with chicken wire.

"Uncle Ned, don't you think it is important that those kids are vindicated? That the church accept responsibility, not just for the removal of those boys from their families but for allowing a minister to continue practicing long after the rumours were spread around?" Ganan had difficulty in staying silent.

"Bringing it up now would just harm more families in the town," his uncle explained. "Those other men had wives and children, some of the townsfolk who knew what went on would have felt guilty, and their children would be tarnished by these revelations. But most importantly, my dad requested that the church's secrets remain hidden, and I for one intend to abide by his wishes. He refused to be shamed."

Stuart intervened at this point, having taken a great deal of interest in the conversation. He loved uncovering pieces of history, and in his younger days, he would have loudly voiced his discoveries. Age had mellowed him and given him a greater understanding of how past deeds can affect future generations. Some things were just better left alone.

"As I said, Ganan, there is nothing really to stop you buying the land and renovating the old church, if you toe the line. I mean the covenant can be lifted if Ned agrees, and I can do the inspections necessary on the building. I find it rather exciting to think of a museum built over old bones." His delight was obvious.

"And we can still give those lost boys a little bit of pride, because we can tell the story of their tormented lives, minus the murder, and let people know how well they did in their jobs, how they saved their money and bought the land, how mental depression, through no fault of their own, finally took their lives. Only Tommy went on to marry and raise children, but he also suffered socially and psychologically, didn't he, Ned?"

Stuart continued, not waiting for Ned's answer. "I think their story needs to be told eventually. They were teased at school, considered too black to be in the front of school photos, probably not believed by the parishioners, and therefore they saw no reason to tell of their torment, just to have the blame put back on themselves. We need to tell why they turned away from religion and how they would have benefited from knowing the culture of their parents up north."

"Ganan," Ned explained to Sylvi's boy, his pseudo nephew, "try to understand that I never told anyone because of respect for my father and because I could see that no good would come of it. I put it at the back of my mind and didn't think about it for many years. Then all the news stories about institutionalized child abuse came out and reminded me, making me rather sad."

"Then you do need to tell someone, Uncle Ned. You always told me that the truth comes out eventually. However, I really want to buy the land and would rather avoid any hassles over unearthed bones. Maybe we can put off the truth for a while longer, get the old church renovated and turned into a museum, put houses or factories on the land, and just keep on with our lives. When everything is settled, maybe we can reveal the old church's secrets."

The two older men had already made up their minds that silence was in the best interests of everyone, and Sylvi did not hesitate to agree. Ganan would get his land, and he knew Jordy well enough to know that a piece of the property would ensure his co-operation.

As he drove slowly past the church on his way home, Ganan could have sworn he saw a face peering through the chicken-wired window. He shook his head and whispered into the dark. "Leave it be, Ganan. Leave it be."

Gabby's Dad

Gabby is a late starter. Single mother, uni graduate, liaison officer, petite, blonde, and blue-eyed, constantly on the go organizing local events and sorting out other people's problems. She is also very proud of her Aboriginal heritage, although that was a matter she had previously ignored, giving it little thought until after she had reached her early thirties. Gabby left her Tasmanian family a few years back to settle in this regional village where her work is well regarded by the townsfolk.

We sat in the same café I had so often shared with Kyle, munching on homemade muffins and sipping rich, aromatic coffees with exotic names. The little café had changed owners since my last visit, but the rustic bentwood chairs and distressed pine tables remained the same. The clientele seemed familiar, or perhaps it was just their manner of dressing in retro clothes and strappy sandals that made them appear that way.

Gabby brought me some paperwork that she had recently received from her family in Tasmania. It was her father's handwritten story, set neatly on the lined sheets of a lecture pad and divided into the memorable phases of his life. As Gabby handed it across the table, her sleeve slid up to reveal a newly purchased tattoo on her forearm: an eagle feather coloured in red, black, and yellow, the colours of the Aboriginal flag. The artist had used his obvious skills to draw soft, fluffy down on the shaft base and beautiful brown stripes across the vane that tightened closer to the tip. It fitted perfectly on Gabby's arm and complimented the feather tattoo on her other forearm.

The feather to me is a symbol of flight, and it passed my mind that Gabby was flying away, running from something. But no, Gabby had already landed and had her feet well and truly on solid ground. She just has a thing about feathers, and I think that perhaps for her it represents freedom, a form of escape from past restrictions that had governed her life. She may have had a problem with identity in the past, but that had long gone. These days, she encourages others to embrace their heritage, whatever that may be, taking the good with the bad and learning resilience along the way.

As I read her father's story, I could see that she had inherited his ability to put things in their place and get on with life. He had survived a difficult and disrupted childhood, moving from town to town and often missing school, with alcohol abuse playing a major part in his family life. Relationships with his kin remained strong, and he greatly admired the strengths exhibited by his hardworking relatives. His wonderful story was addressed to his daughter who, like him, worked hard to achieve a satisfying, fruitful life, regardless of past financial and social setbacks.

Gabby believes her father's story should be told, and although his abbreviated version leaves out the intricate detail of an Indigenous family's life in Tasmania, it hints at adventure, love and duty, and humour amidst the hardship. For a man who had little in the way of formal education, his narrative is surprisingly fluid. I found the occasional nuances and inconsistencies in grammar and expression rather entrancing and would hesitate to change them in any way.

This is how he told his life story to his daughter before he died

Growing Up in Tasmania

> Mum and Aunty Em were in maternity at the same time. Aunt Em gave birth to a baby girl which died, and Mum gave birth to my brother. Mum, so I am told, died while boarding the mail bus to go home. Mum and the baby girl were buried on the same day in Ulverstone Cemetery.
>
> Aunt Em breastfed my brother in hospital. I do not know when he was taken in by the family. I do know that Dad spent some time up in the Mallee country after that. I'm told that the girl (later to be my stepmother), aged fourteen,

was sitting on the mailbox holding me and waiting for Mum and my brother. It was the bus driver who had to break the sad news. I'm pretty sure the bus driver was from the Nietta General Store.

Earliest memories (between Three and Four years old)

My earliest memories are of Grandfather C driving the cows in for milking which was done by hand. The cows were belly deep in mud, there was no concrete and no electric power. Grandfather's dog Rough (a Smithfield) died one night on the porch during a thunderstorm. I remember making myself vomit by drinking warm cream from the milk separator while Grandfather was separating. The separator is, or was, a hand operated machine and when wound over at the correct speed would divide the milk from the cream, milk out the larger spout and cream from the smaller spout.

One day, there seemed to be lots of people eating there. I was in a cot with very high sides and wanted a wee-wee very bad but was afraid to ask and piddled the bed. Auntie Merle scolded me harshly. She was a very severe lady of the church. After leaving Grandfathers I lived with her and her husband on their farm and went to Sunday school every Sunday. Auntie gave me a good smacking one day for crying till I held my breath.

They had three daughters and one was about my age. We captured a black chook and put it in an old oven behind a shed to see if it would lay an egg for us. Naturally we forgot about it and sure got a paddling when it was found dead some weeks later.

The South Nietta schoolteacher was tall, stern and always in black like an undertaker. He and Auntie Merle used to have lots of conversations at the front gate.

Five to Six years old

I don't remember anything for a while, but Dad and step mum were married. Dad had us two boys and Mum had Graeme. We lived on an old deserted farm. Dad had his bullocks then. My brother did not live with us but came for holidays at that time. We got a belting for calling a lady Old Feathery Legs.

One winter, everything was frozen and we went skating. We got our trousers wet. We took them off and continued skating wearing only shoes and shirts. We got sprung and were in trouble again.

My brother, or Shorty as he was mostly called, was very good with his teeth. One day we were lighting fires, carrying bunches of burning bracken fern from place to place to light more. I lit my bunch from one of his fires and was accused of stealing Shorty's fire. We had a boyish punch-up, and I ended with my left thumb in Shorty's mouth. When I did get away he was spitting out a mouthful of my blood. I still have two clear teeth marks on my left shoulder and most likely a full set on my backside but I cannot see there. One day, we were playing in turns going head first though a hole in an old hessian bed. I got ahead of Shorty and took his turn but did not make it. He sank his teeth in my bum and held on like a bull terrier.

When we moved towns, Shorty came to live with us. He really surprised me one day. The boy used his fist and gave me a real beauty in the mouth. I ran yelling and spitting blood to Mum and was told "Don't be such a bloody sook go back and finish the fight." I can't remember if I did or not. Somewhere around nine years old was the last punch up we had I think. Perhaps we had found better pastimes. Shanghais, bows and arrows, and we developed our own kind of gun from the crossbow system and used pointed lengths of plain wire, dangerous to about twenty metres. We shot parrots, cockatoos, rabbits, fish and snakes etc.

Family life, late 1930s and 1940s

Our home (company owned) was constructed of rough sawn timber, no paint. It was lined inside with hessian bags. There was no ceiling, we could lie in bed and watch rats climbing around the rafters. We had a kerosene lamp in the kitchen otherwise lighting was by candle light. We had no newspaper or radio. There was one open fireplace with a wooden chimney and no cooking stove. Water was from a well about a hundred yards from the house, and was carried in four-gallon kerosene tins of water for bath and washing. For washing, the water was boiled in a wood fired copper. While boiling in the copper, the washing was agitated with a piece of wood and then scrubbed on a washing board (a square piece of corrugated glass in a wooden frame). We did not have pillowslips or sheets on our bed. Pillows and mattresses were stuffed with a substance called flak, which always seemed to form into hard uncomfortable lumps. Sometimes there would be five of us in one double bed. From memory I think there was more fighting than sleeping done at that time.

Dad had an excellent method of getting a confession out of us. Taking a firm grip on the ear and slowly twist this member, in a short time it would be of great relief to tell the truth. One day, Shorty was getting the treatment. "Did he have any tobacco in his pocket?" He took a lot of pain before confessing. I was sitting on a potato sack in front of the fire at this time and managed to slide my pinch of tobacco under the sack before my turn and happily turned my pockets out. (I was a good boy wasn't I?)

There were no fat people around in those days as the Government kept wages down to 30 per cent below the cost of living. Sometimes Dad would work for a saw miller for up to three months and find that the miller did not have money to pay him. This led to a chain reaction. He could not pay the grocery store or for the horse food. All purchases seemed to be made on tick or on the slate (credit).

Ted's Hotel in Derby had a large blackboard behind the bar on which were the names of at least half the town, and how much each owed for grog.

Now drinking goes back a long way with our mob and friends. There would always be arguments and usually fights. After a drinking bout Dad would go right out of his tree and take on the wardrobe in the bedroom with boots and fists. In the end the old cupboard was just matchwood.

One booze session took place at Loyetea. I don't remember how long it lasted. One of Dad's mates, Lenny, took bets that on hands and knees he could outfight a blue heeler dog. He got the dog angry by biting its ears and nose. The dog of course tried to escape but could not as Lenny was holding its front leg. It did retaliate, and as Lenny had taken his shirt off for the battle, his face, arms and shoulders were just a bloody, chewed up mess. Needless to say the dog won the fight. With no doctor or medication, Lenny remained out of sight for over a week, and then just turned up at work as normal.

One period when my sister was three to four years old, Dad would like to show his drinking mates just how tough his eldest daughter was. Taking a handful of hair on top of her head he would walk around carrying her like that, drinking and talking to his mates. She did not cry or ever complain.

One of my Uncles brought me my first beer in the Waratah Hotel.

I think I was about eight years old.
That time covered part of the Great Depression and war years. There was no sport or entertainment as is known today. In one respect, I was more fortunate than the others. At Xmas, I would get to visit Auntie Merle and Uncle in Ulverstone and would see a movie at the cost of five pence. We did have pocket money. Once a month we would get one shilling, which would purchase one can of condensed milk and two pence worth of lollies, but not every month.

Food

Often in short supply, kangaroo and wallaby supplemented the meat supply. We did not get fruit or green vegetables except one year when Dad made a garden on the dung heap (horse dung). It was very good but never repeated.
Where we lived at the time was a true rainforest, there was no cleared land at all. The ground was water logged, and roads were made from sawn timber, two or three boards each side of a vehicle. When covered with frost or snow a truck would simply slide sideways off the road and have to be hauled back on again with horses.
There were a few hens and sometimes a cow which often did not get milked, as we could not always find it in the bush. Many meals were made up of small round potatoes cut in half and fried in the pan. Camp oven food was great, mostly a few potatoes, roo, wallaby, plover, parrots, etc. all cooked together. With bread we could have butter or jam but not together. For jam, we had a choice of melon and ginger or melon and pineapple.
Many people made an existence from wild game. Trapping possum and ring-tail possum, brush-tail possum and rock possum, snaring kangaroo and wallaby, trapping rabbits—all

just for their skins which had a ready market. This was a very cruel occupation. Trap lines were tended every third day. As a boy I was involved in this myself. If an animal was trapped, it had a broken leg or snared it would hang by a leg. At least half would be dead on collection and skinning day. Today such cruelty is not tolerated, but then it was accepted as a normal way of life.

Country toilets

Country toilets in some areas up to the late 1960s were very basic. The better class was a hole dug in the ground, usually two feet by three feet and six feet deep (approximately two metres), with a piece of timber, usually round, on which one sat. The most obnoxious was the four-gallon (twenty-litre) can over which was placed a wide board with a bum sized hole cut in it. Toilet paper was torn newspaper. The stench and blowflies on a hot day was truly intolerable. Phenyl, when available, was of some help, as it has its own strong smell. Gabby, if you can remember one such toilet was at Irishtown. The best of all was the much-used open bush, using grass or bracken fern for toilet paper.

School

The school bus was a very dilapidated affair. Due to petrol rationing the engine ran on gas, provided by burning charcoal in a large cylinder or tank mounted on the rear of the vehicle. This method was very ineffective and lacked any sort of power. Going up a steep hill it was quite possible to walk beside the bus and keep pace with it. Anyone who misbehaved was put off and had to walk home anyway. The bus could not get within two miles of the sawmill, so that was a walking job. Food supplies for the four families who lived there came on the bus and we had to carry them home too.

School days started with a line-up and inspection of shoes, fingernails and ears. Did not worry me much as I was seldom there. At thirteen and a half years, my book came home with a message from the headmaster that as I was seldom at school I may as well stay home altogether. When due for a caning we would rub our hand with pine resin to reduce the pain. (It did not work.)

Yes, even in those far days most boys carried a pocketknife. I had a U Beaut Joseph Rodgers that Dad had given me. The bullyboy stole it from me and I found out, so we were fighting over the knife. A teacher came along. He confiscated the knife and a week later returned it to me. In a paddock backing the school ground was a very old horse. Bullyboy caught the old horse one lunch break and forced it to gallop, belting it all the while. The headmaster—to make up his salary, he used to dig potatoes for farmers on weekends and holidays—saw him and caned him so hard that the flesh burst from the ends of his fingers. He was home for a week after. There were no complaints from his parents or anyone. This was accepted as just punishment for his cruelty to the horse.

Now don't think that Shorty and I were bad kids. Sometimes we felt like a good laugh, like chasing the girls around the school yard with a live snake. Or giving someone a matchbox full of big black ants that were agitated, of course, so they would really sting, saying the match box had cigarette butts in it. Tobacco was rationed and the butts were much prized by adults as well as kids. Mum could bribe us into almost anything for a cigarette butt. Or if we were doing a good job in the bush Dad would leave his old bluey coat on a log with a couple of butts in the pocket, so we could pinch them. We went to a lot of schools, often only for a few weeks. A period in the bush near Waratah, there was no school at all.

Easter shooting

At age ten to eleven, I was considered old enough to go on the Easter hunt with Dad and his mates. The first night stop we all slept on the floor of an old hut with no blankets but lots of dogs. The favourite roo dog was a beagle-harrier cross for hunters and the runners were greyhound staghounds, also cross-bred with each other.

Good Friday morning at break of day, we began the climb up Black Buff Range. Six men, twenty-five to thirty dogs, and food supply for four days carried in sugar bags, plus many bottles of wine. These blokes must have been tidy people as no wine bottle was ever left behind. Every empty was thrown up in the air and blasted away with shotguns. While the food was very rough, after climbing and walking all day I could have enjoyed anything. Cooking was Abo style with billy tea. I had my first shot with a gun on that trip and it near broke my shoulder. No skins were taken as we had no means to carry them.

Out hunting, the hounds were set free. When getting the scent of a roo they howl all the time, and by listening to the direction of the dogs it is sometimes possible to judge where it will break cover and get in a shot. To shoot a roo on the hop is difficult. The shot must be fired at the top of the arc or feet on the ground any other time it will be a clean miss.

At the end of this hunt, we were met at an old mining camp by Uncle George, Grandma's brother and his son (renowned for their very violent tempers). They brought with them horses for us to get back to base camp. The mountain fog closed in on us. I was riding behind as close as I could and could not see man or horse, just the shine on the horse's shoes as it lifted its feet. Uncle George and his many sons used to breed hunting dogs, to their own rules. Taken hunting three times before turning eight weeks old, if a pup did not show the correct signs at that age, they were hung by the neck and left in the bush.

Grandfathers

Grandfather R used to visit occasionally. Shorty and I did not like his coming. It was our job to keep the horse stables clean. When the old chap arrived, he would first inspect the stables. If he could find a bit of hay or dung in any corner, which he always did, he would make us clean the whole stable over again. Grandfather C did not ever come to visit and I can only guess at the reason.

On one of Grandfather R's visits, when he would have been in his midsixties, a tree fell on him. He was on his back and the tree was lying between his legs and the whole length of his body, he was badly smashed up. Dad did have a car (a Hudson Terraplane) but due to war rationing, he had no petrol. There was no such thing as an ambulance and if there had been there was no way to make contact as we did not have telephones. He was taken to hospital on a timber truck, and as he had to remain on his back, he could not be put in the cabin of the truck. So he was rolled up in a grey blanket and tied on top of the load of timber. He was considered dying, but after three years of exercise and supreme effort, he was walking again. He died at the age of eighty-four. I'm told it was from an overdose of rum, of which he was very fond. In his younger days, he was a bullock driver.

One day, Grandfather was teaching Shorty and me to plait a whip with roo skin cut into long, thin strips. He got me by the shoulder and examined my biceps. He said, "By God, boy, you will have a long life. You've got Indian muscles." Doing the same to Shorty, he made no comment. Just carried on with the lesson.

When the family lived seventeen miles from Ulverstone he would go to town by horse and sulky (the horse's name was Jenny) and get a real skinful of rum. The locals would put him in the sulky, paralytic drunk, and Jenny would take him the seventeen miles home.

His wife Grandma Harriet had waist-length, straight hair. On my few visits there with Shorty, I cannot remember her speaking to me. I believe there was a feud between the two families. I think because Dad married my mother's sister. I'm a bit foggy here as I would have been four to six years at the time, but Grandfather C came home very badly beaten up and remained in bed for over a week. The explanation was that he had been attacked by crows. To me he was a kindly, gentle man and I loved him dearly. After his wife died, he remained a widower and raised his family alone. He must have been a First World War veteran, because he owned a repatriation farm. After his death, his youngest son took on the farm and soon failed. Then his eldest son Richard tried and failed. The land is still there on the west side of the South Nietta Road and backs down to the river but it is now a pine plantation.

All Grandfather C's misfortunes seemed to happen in the month of May. His wife and twelve-year-old daughter both died in May and were buried on the Ulverstone cemetery on the same day. He broke his leg in May, plus many more others, and died in May.

His middle son Uncle Al owned a grey stallion. I would have been about three years old but can still clearly see and hear those hooves lashing out over me. I must have been lying on the ground flat or he would have killed me for sure. Someone, I don't know who, pulled him away from me.

At the outbreak of war Al was seventeen but told the army people he was eighteen and joined the First Second AIF—I think 42nd Battalion. The troop ship he was on was just off the coast of Singapore, which had fallen to the Japanese. They were notified and turned away. He was in Crete, Greece, Borneo, and the Middle East and was a Rat of Tobruk. In the army, he had plenty of chances for promotion. He said that he would lose his mates, and nothing was worth that, so he would deliberately break the rules and spend a lot of time peeling spuds in the mess and in the lock-up.

At the end of war his only physical wound was a bullet graze on his scalp. Of course, he was mentally wounded. He could drink alcohol in huge lots and never show any signs of being drunk. At the end of the war he spent ten years at Tin Can Bay in Queensland, I guess doing his own rehabilitation. In those days, there was no help for mentally disturbed people. Eventually, he returned to Tasmania and was working in the bush using a chain saw when a limb fell from a tree and killed him. He was buried in the Penguin Cemetery with full military honours.

The Xmas before he died I went home for a visit. I counted the empty flagons, eighteen. That is eighteen gallons of wine that Dad and Uncle Al had drunk. I won't attempt to describe the condition of Dad. But Uncle Al, apart from the smell, appeared in every sense to be totally sober.

Work

In 1947, a farmer provided me with twelve dozen rabbit traps to work his farm. These I tended every day and moved them all to a new location every third day. The wage for a worker was five pounds a week at this time. I earned nine pounds a week from skins, but only in the winter months. At the end of the session, I got a job in the sawmill at Loongana. I was around fifteen years old.

Food was provided by the company, Alstergreen and Co. The sleeping quarters was a very large shed, no divisions or partitions, just a big open shed. There were about fourteen of us sleeping in there. After work and weekends we had absolutely nothing to do except to swim in the Leven River.

My transport was a very old push bike (Malvern Star) which Uncle Al had left behind when he went to war. It was seventeen miles to another Uncle's place and thirty-seven miles to Ulverstone. There were no sealed roads from there and back to Uncle's house. Shorty came for a little while. We slept in a shed out back. We had a childish argument over some silly thing one morning and a bit of a punch-up. He took a swing at my head with a bottle. I took it off him and threw it away. I went to the house and had breakfast. When I went out again, Shorty was gone. I did not see him again for many years after that.

I earned two pounds a week and keep. Don't remember if I always got paid or not but there was always a bottle of Gin on Friday nights. Along with the bottle of Gin on Friday nights we used to have boxing (with gloves). Auntie Em used to join in too with the aid of some Gin she was good. Gave me many a good thumping I can tell you. They had four girls. A couple of times, there was a kind of neighbours' nights with a nine-gallon keg (wooden) of beer sat on a stump (no refrigeration then), and a big log fire. We attempted to ride young steers and ended up with heaps of bruises, and a great hangover next morning.

Antill Ponds was halfway between Hobart and Launceston. In our time it was a derelict pub with fourteen bedrooms. There were what looked like bullet holes in the ceiling of the bar room. Dad claimed they were put there by Dan Kelly who was shooting at flies. Of course we did not believe this but on modern information, it is quite possibly true. Also there was a tombstone (can't remember the inscription) against the rail station wall and the lower half of the grave is under the highway.

At Tunbridge, seven miles north of Antill Ponds, I worked for a sawmill cutting logs with a crosscut saw, and earned my first motor car from there. I lived on spuds and butter for three months to raise the eighty pounds to pay for it, a 1928 Chevrolet. Wages were ten pounds a week. I bought it from a friend of Dad's. We met in the Oatlands Hotel. I gave my eighty pounds to pay for it, and he gave me the keys, paperwork. All on a handshake. That was the only time I ever saw this chap.

Also at Tunbridge Mill a man, Lenny, was the benchman (now an obsolete trade) who physically pushed parts of the log through a circular saw and cut it into timber boards to size. Len had seven children to care for. While pushing a flitch (piece of log) through a circular saw he forgot to remove his hand from on top of the flitch. There was a sickening thump, a noise still clear in my memory. The saw took off four fingers and the end of the thumb on his right hand. He staggered backwards and sat down against the wall. He was taken to hospital by car. Len did not pass out. He was fully conscious all the time. When released from hospital after three weeks, he came straight back to work with his right wrist strapped to his left shoulder. Note that at this time there were no benefits, such as work care, the dole, or any other form of help. Life was simple, no work, no pay.

When you hear oldies refer to the good old days, note the only good was that life was simple and uncomplicated, the rest was just a battle for survival. Empty stomachs were quite normal.

Dilgers Mill 1948

Left Derby with Dad and Uncle Richard in a 1936 Bedford Ute to spend a week in the bush cutting logs with the boys. We stopped at Pinegana Pub for a quick beer and left two days later with one hell of a hangover and craving for food. I reckon I could smell that camp oven a mile before getting to the camp. The boys had shot some small wallaby, parrots and native hen, and with a few spuds made a terrific stew. I did not know how to treat such an empty stomach, dug in and ate my fill and paid a painful price with severe diarrhoea for a week after.

Woodsdale about 1949

Got a job in Swan's Sawmill at ten pounds per week. My possessions were a beaten-up pushbike, one grey blanket, one billycan, knife and fork, along with the trousers and shirt I wore. Food to survive the first two weeks to payday included one tomato one large loaf of bread (one slice a day) and I did trap one rabbit and boiled it with the tomato. No pepper, salt or sugar, and no butter. I filled in the menu with spuds I stole after dark from a farmer's paddock. I had a great time in the general store on payday with my twenty pounds. It was probably equal to five hundred dollars today. Life became good again. There were no tanks or fresh water there, water was carted in forty-four-gallon drums and even when boiled tasted of petrol.

Xmas break I pedalled home to Tunack to the very small sandstone cottage called home. All the boys slept in a shed outside. Two of us decided to celebrate Xmas and walked the two miles to the pub. No beer. I think it was 1950, before beer was available after the war. The publican was an inventive chap. He sold Tunack special in Gin bottles. It really packed a punch, a mixture of hard liqueur flavoured with raspberry cordial. Well, we brought a bottle each and walked on home. Last I remember we were sitting on a log singing, and I woke up in bed wearing only my belt. Mum's sister was helping out, and it was her who undressed me and put me to bed. Oh the embarrassment. I could never forget. Like a mongrel dog, I slunk back to Woodvale and spent the holidays alone.

Drysart

Dad secured a logging contract with a Seventh Day Adventist family to supply their sawmill at Austins Ferry (near Hobart) with logs. We arrived on site with seven horses and a beat-up old Ford truck with the driver's door missing. I was the driver. First week, we slept on the ground under the truck until some waste timber arrived to build a camp. Dad's camps only ever had three walls with one end open, but they were surprisingly warm. With our four beds in place there was space of two square metres left for the living area. Beds were made of one chaff bag (hessian) on two round poles, so placed to create a hollow area between them and this space filled with hay and a grey blanket on top. Dad always slept in the foetal position and ground his teeth all night long. He also kept the blanket pulled up over his head.

This camp had no table and no cupboards. Tea from the billycan and cooking in the camp oven. Vegetables were potatoes and swedes, meat was from gun and dog. Flies were kept off the meat by placing a wide board in a hessian bag, tying off the end and hanging the bag so it did not touch anything. Brush-tailed possum is good eating but must be buried in the ground for seven days to remove the strong flavour before cooking. Badger or wombat is not unlike beef to eat. Dad was crazy on Porcupine (echidna), there were no rabbits in the place then.

Now to work, the old bloke must have had night vision as he would arise around 4 a.m., take two horses and truck up the bush, load up with logs, and be back at the camp by 6 a.m. for me to take the load to Austins Ferry. We had no rego or insurance. The tyres on truck and trailer were long unroadworthy by today's standards. With wind-up car jacks and vulcanised patches I mended up to seven punctures to deliver one load of logs. The round trip was around 150 kilometres. With breakdowns and punctures and an average speed of about thirty kilometres, it took sometimes fourteen hours to do one load. I would get back to camp at 2 a.m., but that bloody truck would be loaded and waiting for me at 6 a.m. again.

I can not clearly remember but we were there for several months, food supply for us and the horses was all on credit. But Dad did not get paid at all for this work. He did get a letter from the eldest son of this religious family telling him how wonderful it was to be on an aeroplane leaving Tasmania and up above all his troubles.

James Thomas

One of fourteen children, James was bullock driving at the age of fourteen years, forming his own team of twelve bullocks. The leaders were two Red Devons with massive horns named Lark and Nimble.

In the late 1930s it was found that horses worked single file (usually in teams of seven), were faster and easier to drive in the dense Tasmanian forest than were bullocks. So J. T. then became a horseman, and a champion at that. He worked his teams by voice only and had such control over these animals that they were like an extension of his own body.

> The advent of tractor and chainsaw were devastating to him. Not knowing any other work or trade he held on against the modern evils until he was very deeply in debt. He failed badly at everything else he tried and ended as a nomad and a drunk.

Gabby had grown up hearing brief excerpts of her father's life, sometimes told at the evening meal table or used as examples when he wanted to show his children that they had little to complain about in this day and age. However, even she did not truly understand the hardships endured until they were written down and read as a whole. Her father had learned to accept the difficulties he faced in childhood and during later adult years, simply because it seemed there was no choice. For his children, there were more opportunities, and Gabby seized those chances, moving to the mainland and building on the strengths she had inherited from her hard-living, hard-drinking mob back home.

Almost as an afterthought, her father added a few philosophical lines to finish off his narrative and explain how he managed to mentally survive the turmoil of his past.

> **Dreams**
> What I am now going to write has been true all my life. If I dream of a tree or place, I will see that dream within one moon cycle. If, after dark I hear two plovers fly directly overhead, both making their call, I will have serious trouble the next day. I have probably taken more chances with life and limb than the average person. On many occasions I've had this feeling of danger and never ignored that. Usually afterwards, I've seen evidence that had I ignored this feeling I would have at least been injured.
> When under severe emotional stress I lie on my back on the earth, arms spread. I will leave my body and float face down, arms spread over the earth, varying from a couple of metres

> to several hundred metres. Time has no meaning at all. On return I can face up to whatever the problem may be.

Now I was brought up as a nonbeliever, an atheist in the truest sense of the word, but there was something in that final addition to his story that made me wonder if the spirits of his Indigenous ancestors did perhaps visit and advise during difficult times. Lying on his back on the earth that had nurtured countless generations of his dark-skinned kinfolk, it seemed entirely plausible that their capacity to survive in the cold Tasmanian wilderness for thousands of years could somehow pass into his own modern day soul.

I suspect that Gabby's fascination with feathers and dream catchers is an extension of that spirit world her father occasionally inhabited.

Acknowledgements

Although these stories are works of fiction, there are elements that might be familiar to some readers. I am appreciative of the contributions from many people who have given my characters, along with the towns they live in, a life that could be real and could be recognised in any small community where secrets are kept.

I am especially grateful to Gail Radford for graciously allowing me to use parts of her father's fascinating, difficult life and for her contribution to my own understanding about growing up as an Indigenous person in country Tasmania.

Kyle Jones's telephone conversations and emails were invaluable. His memories came to me at a time when this book seemed to be going nowhere, and I was delighted by his light-hearted attitude to the insults he had endured as a child. His honesty and openness encouraged me to continue writing.

I also want to thank my son Hayden, whose guileless conversations inspired many of the stories.

About the Author

Sandra M. Mallia lives with her husband, close to their ever-increasing family, on the outskirts of Melbourne. She has a Bachelor of Arts degree in professional writing and is currently studying for a Master's in writing. This is her first book.

About the Book

You don't know your neighbourhood until you start asking questions. In this collection of short stories, secrets are revealed and ancestries are uncovered in a progressive, fictional town that lies on the city fringe. Some residents have kept their Indigenous heritage to themselves out of fear that they will be ostracized, while others have simply found it easier to pretend they are white. Some are only just learning of their background and beginning to take pride in a culture that has, up until now, been denied.

These stories are entwined within the fabric of the town. They involve people from all occupations who are often surprised or offended that they, as long-term residents, are unaware of the histories of friends, relatives, or workmates. Relationships are occasionally destroyed, crimes are committed, and mental illness becomes a problem. But more often, the characters gain strength and respect as hidden lives are unearthed and a small-town culture changes with the times.